Although Caroline and her father had hardly been on the best of terms, he had left her a house in tropical Queensland, and it seemed as good a place as any to go and start a new life. But how could she, when the formidable Kiall Stirling was so determined never to let her forget the old scandal about her mother and his uncle Martin?

Books you will enjoy
by MARGARET WAY

A SEASON FOR CHANGE

When Samantha's life fell apart, it was Nico Martinelli who did his best to help her. She had never known anyone quite like Nico—rich, handsome, compelling, and apparently attracted to her. *So why was she so afraid of him?*

THE McIVOR AFFAIR

It wasn't her father who had cheated Drew McIvor, Marnie knew, but her stepmother—yet how could she give her stepmother away? Just as much to the point, how could she kill this feeling of attraction that persisted in growing between her and the hateful Drew?

SHADOW DANCE

When Carl Denning gave her the job of tracking down and interviewing the elusive Richard Kaufmann, Alix was far from pleased—but the assignment led her into helping Richard repair the situation between him and his ex-wife. If only it had also helped her to sort out the troubled situation between herself and Carl!

TEMPLE OF FIRE

Julian Standford had all the autocratic ways of his overbearing family. He was also rich, handsome and charming—when he wanted to be. In short, he had everything. Everything except a heart. But the only way Fleur could be with her beloved young brother again was to live in the same house with Julian and his overwhelming relatives. Could she possibly stand up to them *all*?

NORTH OF CAPRICORN

BY

MARGARET WAY

MILLS & BOON LIMITED
15–16 BROOK'S MEWS
LONDON W1A 1DR

First published 1981
Australian copyright 1981
Philippine copyright 1981
This edition 1981

© Margaret Way 1981

ISBN 0 263 73677 6 -17/33

Set in Monophoto Plantin 10 on 11½ pt.

Made and printed in Great Britain by Richard Clay (The Chaucer Press) Ltd, Bungay, Suffolk

CHAPTER ONE

IT was the first time Ian Randall had ever met his father's young client, and he was still recovering from the shock. For one thing, though she was only seventeen years old and quite alone, she had a look of detachment that was almost incongruous in a schoolgirl. Fairly well briefed on her lonely background, he had expected her to be painfully shy, not a collected young beauty staring him in the eye. Even a hideous school uniform and no make-up could not hide that. When he could stand her gaze no longer, iridescent green eyes between heavy black lashes, he began to apologise in what he hoped was a friendly tone, but came out treacly pompous.

'A pity my father had to get the 'flu. A bit awkward. I realise, of course, you'd be a lot happier dealing with him.'

'If you'd just *tell* me, Mr Randall.' The young voice was courteous enough, but as severe as her expression, cutting off what he later thought of as his 'waffling'.

'The fact is, Caroline,' he used her Christian name, not as a kindness, but to reduce her to a child, 'there *is* no easy way to tell you. It's my sad duty to tell you your father has passed away.'

It would have astonished him if she had cried. She didn't even drop her iridescent eyes. 'When?'

He frowned down at the papers on his desk. 'As I have it—Tuesday morning. Heart attack, it says here.'

'No matter—he's dead.'

For an instant he could think of absolutely nothing

to say, then he tut-tutted. 'Really, Caroline!' Such callousness was shocking.

'It's very difficult to hold on to memories, Mr Randall,' she said quietly. 'I haven't seen my father since I was eight years old. Since I was abandoned.'

'There were circumstances. . . .' He turned quickly to defending their late client.

'Of course.' There was a bored look on her face as though she had to force herself to listen to his babbling. 'It's even possible I could have understood had I ever been told. What, if anything, did he leave me?'

'What's that?' Reluctantly he softened his gaze. Her features were perfection, small and chiselled like a statue's but without life or warmth.

'I said,' she repeated seriously, 'what did my father leave me?'

'Enough.' He was betrayed into speaking more curtly than he intended. Her attitude was making him feel anything but kindhearted. 'I have his will here.'

'Then perhaps you could read it.'

'I shall do so.' He gave the words a quelling emphasis. What an unnerving girl! His father might have warned him.

She sat quite still while he droned through the legal document and when he finally looked up from his desk, he was amazed to find her eyes blazing.

'Do you mean to tell me I own a *house*?'

The change in her was as bewildering as it was dazzling; from icy to glittering. She didn't seem at all interested in the money.

'Not much of an asset, Caroline,' he pointed out with all earnestness. 'An isolated farmhouse in North Queensland. The property hasn't been worked for well over a year when the last tenant left.'

'But still—a house!' She drew a ragged breath and

he heard it. 'Do you know how my father came by it?'

'Why, I understand he was born there,' he said, startled.

'But that's impossible!' She shook her ash-blonde head as though there was something terribly wrong. 'He was born in Africa—Kenya.'

'No,' he rejected that emphatically, almost glad to prove her wrong. 'He merely lived there for a good part of his life, had his business there. It was sold up some months ago. Your father must have been aware of the seriousness of his condition. His affairs were put carefully in order.'

'All except me.' A flicker of something like desolation crossed her face and was quickly gone. 'But then I was never a part of his life.'

'You mustn't say that, Caroline,' he stared back at her thoughtfully, forcing himself to feel sympathy. 'He left you everything he had.'

'I'm sorry, but I would have much preferred his love.' She spoke quietly, yet her young voice seemed to ring around the room.

Love, the dreary word that seemed to pepper women's conversation. 'I'm sure he loved you in his own way,' he declared smoothly, not wanting to witness a sudden show of passion. 'You've had a first-class education and there's money. Not a fortune by any means, but enough to set you comfortably on your feet.'

'Then I'll go North.'

For the first time he felt alarm and showed it. 'But, my dear girl. . . .' she might just as well have said she was going off to live with a native tribe. 'What about university? I seem to recall my father's saying you're an excellent student.'

'And why not?' The green eyes were not flattered,

but ironic. 'Studies are all I've ever had. Not enjoyable really to spend vacations studying. I can go to university if I want, when I want, but for now, I'm going up to Queensland to see my property.'

'But there'll be nothing for you there!' He spread out his hands almost pleadingly. 'Nothing! Your youth, your sex—everything goes against you. Think it out, Caroline. Speak to my father. Another week should see him up and about. Young ladies aren't supposed to go haring off to the tropics.'

'I'm going all the same.' There was a lifetime of determination in her tone, a hundred related factors. 'How soon can you arrange for me to get some money?'

So at last she was coming to the money. 'My father has been appointed your legal guardian until you reach the age of eighteen,' he told her warningly.

'Which is all of a few months away.' She threw him a green, sardonic glance. 'I like your father. *He's* always been kind to me. I'm sure he won't object if I at least have a look at the place that belongs to me. I've never had anything, you know, but a bed in a girl's dormitory.'

Ian dared not think of her in a bed, especially at a time like this. One didn't expect such sexuality from a schoolgirl, subtle but powerful, or was he imagining it?

'Surely you had friends to invite you away?' Why was he needling her? Poor little beggar.

'I've always hated pity.'

'Perhaps you're really a loner?' And an arrogant little devil.

'I suppose I am,' she said perilously like humbly, 'but I never sought it.' She closed her eyes for a moment in a curiously weary gesture, then opened them looking across at the young solicitor. 'In another fortnight I'll have left my schooldays behind me for ever. I hated my old life. Now I'm going to write my own future.'

'Then don't be rash.' He was very much taken aback. 'You don't really see yourself as a farmer, do you?' So absurd when she looked like a puff of wind would blow her away.

'I daresay I could have a go at it.'

'Sugar cane?' He almost but not quite drawled a contemptuous *darling*.

'Oh, it's sugar?'

'You'd expect it, wouldn't you, from North Queensland? It's all sugar.'

'A wealth of primary industry, actually,' Caroline corrected him, not for nothing top of the class. 'Timber, tea, tobacco, all the tropical fruits. North Queensland is one of the richest areas for livestock production anywhere in Australia—and just think of those minerals! The North is a treasure house. Brilliant.'

'A lot of it's an unmapped wilderness,' he pointed out a little vigorously. 'Jungle—and it must be hell in the Wet. They're coming into the cyclone season as you well know. I wouldn't care to be blown out to sea.' For an instant it was as if he really saw himself swept to his death.

'One of our boarders lives in Cairns,' she suddenly said, and laughed. 'She's accepted the cyclones for all the beauty of the tropics. Rain forests and gorges slicing through the mountains, the lure of the Reef and the coral islands. I think the tropics might not be too bad at all. Why are you staring at me?' she asked abruptly.

'I beg your pardon.' All in all, he had had enough of her, with her blonde hair and her green eyes, the beauty rising above the traditional ghastly schoolgirl gear. 'In practice I think you'd find it over-rich. In any case you can't slip awaywithout first speaking to my father. He'll be anxious to have a little talk.'

'Could you possibly arrange something next week?' If she was conscious of his disapproval she gave no sign of it, though she had to be, from the glint in her eyes. 'The week after I'll be deprived of my foundling home.'

There was a tap at the door and as Ian looked up Dorothy Creevey, his father's secretary looked in encouragingly.

'It suddenly struck me that you might like a cup of tea?'

'Caroline?' Ian said, understanding Dorothy might think the girl had to be fussed over.

'No, thank you. I don't really like it.'

He conceded her a superior smile. 'I expect if you go North you'll find yourself drinking it silly.'

Behind them, Dorothy wondered unhappily what was wrong.

CHAPTER TWO

THE North shocked her; the heat and the colour, the way the giant sugar cane encroached on the town. One got the feeling it could rise up and devour them all. Stirling was a large town, yet Caroline was amazed and unappreciative of the way everyone was ambling around in a state of undress.

A Eurasian girl went by, her beauty breathtaking, the merest wisp of a bandeau around her breasts, shorts so short, that without the girl's body looking so beautiful they would have been horrible. The Lord only knew what Sister Bonaventure would have said:

I can't bear it, she thought. Overdressed for the tropics, her whole body was aflame with the heat. The town was very pleasant, she could see that, with an engagingly exotic air, but not for a moment did she think it was civilised. No one, for instance, wore a decent pair of shoes.

Of course they're staring at me. Tourists were becoming less frequent with the dreaded monsoon just around the corner, but the locals had clearly marked her for a 'city slicker'. Throughout her long journey, thousands of miles from her old boarding school in stately Melbourne, her spirits had been soaring like a phoenix from the flames. Now she was tired and positively irritable, longing for a shower. If Ian Randall were here now he would certainly be crowing. Her green eyes glittered as she thought of him. On the night before her departure he had actually taken her out to dinner, and unless she was going mad, his manner had been vaguely amorous. None of the nuns had approved, but little Sister Lucy had summoned up a smile at the end, telling Caroline she looked charming when she knew she looked a fright.

Defeated, Caroline slumped down on a bench outside the bus station and pulled her long blonde hair into a makeshift topknot. Tendrils cascaded down, but what the devil! Normally such untidiness would have infuriated her, but she realised sadly, the heat was getting to her. She had never experienced such humidity in her life. Formidable, like a giant hand wringing her out.

From the direction of the picturesque hotel, a nuggety little man approached at a snail's pace, took one look at Caroline, almost hysterical with discomfort, and sat down beside her.

'Stranger here, I reckon?' he said airily.

'Yes.' Because of the circumstances of her life Caroline was anything but communicative, and that 'yes' was very discouraging.

'I could tell,' he said with a quiver of pleasure. 'Gee whizz, I've never seen anything like your skin!'

'Perhaps you can tell me where I can get a taxi.' said Caroline, determined to keep all communication to a minimum.

'Well now, where are you going'?' He was peering at her intently.

'The Mackenzie place.' That was how old Mr Randall had described it.

'That old dump!' the little man whistled in his chest. 'What would you be doin' there? It's deserted.'

'It's not now,' she said, tight-lipped as Mother Superior. 'It's mine.'

'Well, I never!'

An awestruck silence from him while Caroline

tipped back her head in the baleful heat and tried for a
breeze.

'Let's get this straight, girlie,' the little man said
urgently, 'have you bought the place?'

'The fact is, I've been left it,' Caroline managed at
last. Pants, she realised now, were much too hot for
the tropics. Her legs were suffocating inside synthetic.

'My goodness!' The little man scratched his shiny
nut-brown pate. 'Be a good girl and tell me your
name.'

There was a peculiar note in his voice that made her
answer him when all her life she had been taught not
to talk to strange men. 'Marshall,' she said languidly.
'Caroline Marshall.'

To her astonishment, he leaned forward and clapped
her on the shoulder. 'You're *not* Teddy Marshall's girl?'

It was unthinkable that her father had ever been
called Teddy. 'My father's name was Edward,' she told
him in Sister Bonaventure's sharply silencing tone.

'Gawd almighty!' The little man stared at her
aghast.

'That wasn't even his second name,' Caroline gave
him a wintry smile.

The little man ignored her, pulling out a pair of anci-
ent-looking spectacles, resplendent with a safety pin,
and sticking them on his nose. 'Surely your dad's not
dead, then?'

'Just so,' Caroline said brusquely with a strange
inner pain. Events were pointing to a hasty shift.

'Well, I never!' The little man appeared greatly
upset. 'Some people ya can't kill with an axe and others
just get up and die.'

There was no way she could deny this remarkable
statement. Her lungs were aching just trying to take
breath.

'If you could just tell me where the cabs are?'

'We don't have much around 'ere in the way of cabs, girlie. I'll drive you out to the house meself. I had a feelin' I knew ya right away. Your dad damn nearly killed me once. Of course, it was a little joke.'

'Some joke!' She hoped he wasn't going to inflict on her the whole story. Not now, at any rate. She was so weary, yet churned up.

'I really oughta know you,' the little man sighed. 'I'm Paddy, of course.'

'Of course.' Caroline looked pleadingly at the burning blue sky.

'Just like your dad,' he wheezed. 'A smart alec.'

Caroline looked down and around at him startled. 'Was he?'

'Don't ya know?' It was Paddy's turn to be startled.

'No.' It seemed unthinkable now to tell him her father had dumped her on the mercy of the nuns at the tender age of eight.

'A tragedy about your mum,' Paddy said with deepest sympathy. 'The prettiest girl I ever saw.'

Jacaranda blossoms spilled down on Caroline's head and she brushed them off irritably. 'You mean she lived here?'

'Only for a little while.' Paddy's fuzzy eyes were turned inward. 'They were a terrific-lookin' couple, your dad so big and handsome and your little mum like an angel come to earth. That's how I always thought of her—an angel come to earth.'

If I stay another minute, I'll faint, Caroline thought dazedly. Paddy's disclosures were having a shattering effect on her. Her mother had died giving her birth, and when she had been little she had always thought this was the reason her father was so cross with her.

'Are you all right, love?' Paddy was asking her in a voice of the utmost concern.

'Look, you wouldn't care to drive your car over?'

'Not a car really.' Paddy's tone was apologetic. 'It's a ute.'

'So long as it gets me home I'll be happy.'

'But, love, there'll be no electricity or anything. Poor old Salvo couldn't cope. On top of everythin' the grass is a mile high. You'll have snakes thrashin' about everywhere.'

'*Snakes?*' On the narrow bench Caroline began to shake. A dump was one thing, but snakes would push her beyond her limit. No such parallel situation had touched her in her life.

'Nuthin' for it but to see Mr Stirling,' Paddy exclaimed. 'I mean, the place isn't exactly fit for a young lady.'

'I'll get it cleaned up tomorrow,' Caroline said with resolution. Why hadn't she thought of snakes? It was the tropics, after all. She felt a terrible lurch of horror, but quickly quelled it. Surely she had read somewhere that if you left snakes alone they would keep to their side of the bargain. No event in her life had ever been painless.

Just as Paddy was looking down at her unhappily, a big, gaunt woman in an incredible garment surged towards them and addressed Paddy in a voice of ferocity.

'Surely you're not worrying this pretty little gel here?' The accent was British Empire, extraordinarily intimidating.

'Who, me?' Paddy demanded indignantly, a monkey to a giraffe. 'I'm tryin' to help her out of a pack of trouble.'

'Rubbish!' the woman looked at Caroline with mag-

nificent dark eyes and for an instant Caroline thought
it was Sister Bonaventure standing right there. 'Joyce
Coddington, m'dear. Paddy might not be bothering
you, but you're clearly in need of help.'

Habits die hard. Caroline found herself on her feet
respectfully. 'Caroline Marshall, Mrs Coddington.'

Paddy stifled a guffaw. '*Miss.*'

'By choice, Patrick Murphy.' Miss Coddington took
Caroline's hand and gripped hard. 'The heat getting to
you, m'dear?'

'It is rather.' Caroline wondered why Miss Coddington could look so crazy yet so dauntingly superior.

'You'll get used to it, only you have to dress
properly.'

'Like you, Joycie?' Paddy threw in with gleeful
malice.

Obviously Miss Coddington was used to it, for she
ignored him. 'Surely you're not sightseeing in the pre-
Wet?' She regarded Caroline with calm surprise.

'Cheer up, Joycie, she's come here to live.'

'You remind me of someone.' Miss Coddington's
gaunt, distinguished face contorted with concentration.

'Give 'er time!' Paddy spoke to the flagging girl with
a measure of pride in Miss Coddington's accomplish-
ments.

'For God's sake . . .' Miss Coddington looked
alarmed, 'you're not. . . .'

'Take it easy, Joycie.'

'The Marshall child?' Miss Coddington finished.

'I regret to say I am.' Caroline, feeling half dead
tottered back to the bench again.

'For God's sake!' Miss Coddington sounded
appalled.

'There's a bit to straighten out, Joycie,' Paddy exclaimed. 'Teddy's dead.'

'*Dead?*' Miss Coddington joined Caroline on the bench. 'I always knew he'd meet a violent end. Paddy,' she suddenly snapped at the little man, 'go and fetch your vehicle. I'm taking this child home.'

'No.' In an instant Caroline's torpor was entirely gone. 'It's very kind of you, Miss Coddington, but I'm going to the farm.'

'I fear, m'dear, you don't know what you're saying.'

'It's too hot to argue,' Paddy smiled at Caroline encouragingly. 'Joycie's got a damn fine place, perched right on top of the 'ill.'

'It's a matter of belonging,' Caroline explained.

'Then there's nothing for it but to take the child home,' Miss Coddington said quietly after a few moments of studying the girl's bleak expression. 'I really can't bear to sit in your old utility, Paddy, but I'll come.' Miss Coddington drew herself up to a drop under six feet and glanced down at Caroline, who stood up with uncharacteristic meekness. 'Lead on, Paddy.'

They lurched all the way out to the farmhouse, so close together that Caroline felt absolutely rotten.

'You'd be much better off with Joycie, believe me,' Paddy told her. 'The old farm could never be 'ome to ya. For *one* thing. . . .'

'That's enough, Paddy!'

'Yes, Joycie.' Paddy bent even more closely over the wheel. 'The bloody place'll be jungle!'

'Isn't it all?' Caroline spoke a shade wildly.

A scant few hundred yards clear of the town and the wilderness had set in; a landscape so different from what Caroline had ever seen, she felt dwarfed and threatened. In the background the purple ranges, covered in rain forest, the wealth of the sugar crop that

lined the road in virulent green, blood red fields lying
fallow, magnificent blossoming trees of every kind and
colour, Madagascan and South American giants
planted by the early settlers, Cuban Royal Palms,
stands of the great fan-shaped travellers' trees and
cabbage palms, dazzling displays of vines that sprawled
over anything horizontal and even climbed to the tops
of the great palms; an incredible vista of vegetation
like paradise gone mad. Any minute she expected to
encounter a herd of charging buffalo or a sign that
said: look out for the crossing crocodiles.

'Gorgeous, isn't it?' Miss Coddington exclaimed
blissfully, in her wonderfully resonant voice. 'I
wouldn't live anywhere else. Of course my family have
written me off, but I found it very tame at home. Any
fool can hang about and pour tea. Personally I'm all
for colour! Last frontiers and adventure.'

Paddy cackled loudly. 'Mad dogs and Englishmen
go out in the noonday sun.'

'Probably,' Miss Coddington admitted. 'Just one
more little bend and we're home.'

Caroline sought for another word and couldn't find
it. The farmhouse looked as if it had surrendered every
last claim to civilisation to the jungle. She all but
slumped back in horror.

'My goodness isn't the magnolia tree lovely!' Miss
Coddington cried, and got out, adjusting her peacock-
hued draperies.

'It seems to be holding up the house,' Caroline commented.

'Now you know why I didn't like to bring ya.' Paddy
caught the look in her big green eyes.

'No matter—we'll get it right.' Miss Coddington
quelled him with a glance. 'Chop, chop! Get out.'

Caroline dragged herself out and stared about her

with astonishment. 'Didn't the last tenant at least try?'

'Shoulda been arrested!' Paddy exclaimed. 'It's supposed to be haunted.'

Miss Coddington swung around aghast, got a strong grip on the little man and shook him. 'Whatever do you use for sense?'

'How should I know!' Ineffectually Paddy tried to pull away. 'The kid's gotta hear the stories.'

Miss Coddington gave him another shake, looking towards Caroline who wasn't even bothering to disguise her horror.

Once it might have been a romantic tropical bungalow. A timber structure elevated on stumps, surrounded by verandahs to provide deep shade for the central core, the delicate iron lace balustrading and the fretwork at the top of the capitals extraordinarily attractive. Now it looked like the next monsoon would push it over, the timber stumps veering to the left. On all sides the monstrous vegetation crowded the building, the magnolia with great flowers like dinner plates supporting it on one side, the showiest tree she had ever seen in her life, the poinciana, huddled over it like an umbrella, on the other. What there had been of a cultivated garden had gone back to the wild. It was like a mad canvas splashed with every conceivable colour.

'Shall we go up?' said Miss Coddington in a voice determined to press on.

Paddy bit back a retort.

'Nothing to it without a key.' Caroline was beginning to feel quite unreal.

'Paddy will get in, won't you, Paddy?'

Paddy closed his eyes.

When Paddy finally clambered through a window and admitted them to the house, Caroline shrank back at the odour, a compound of very oppressive scents.

'The place just needs airing,' Miss Coddington said, and made a sweep at some curtains that immediately fell down. 'Men aren't exactly the best housekeepers, and to make matters worse Salvo used to drink.'

'Gone troppo,' Paddy confirmed, and patted a sofa cosily. 'I tell ya what we'll do. Go back with Joycie and I'll organise a little working bee.'

'It's all right,' Mr Murphy,' Caroline said gallantly, 'I'm looking forward to doing it all myself.'

'God forbid!' Miss Coddington came back from sweeping through the rooms. 'One thing is certain, you can't stay here tonight.'

'Is there electricity?' Paddy asked.

'Curiously enough, yes. Probably Salvo never notified them to turn it off.' She touched a finger to a dusty cabinet and clicked her tongue disgustedly. 'It's important in the tropics not to let oneself go.'

'Take Joycie, for instance,' said Paddy.

Caroline could sense the kindness in these two widely disparate people, but now she was nervous and wanted to be alone. There were a few redeeming features. Fruit seemed to grow in abundance; mangoes almost bowed to the ground, luscious hands of bananas, avocados she could probably acquire a taste for, a laden pawpaw tree. No need to go hungry, and all she felt like was something very light. It didn't even occur to her; most girls would have been petrified at the thought of staying alone.

'Dug your toes in, have you?' said Miss Coddington, sank down in an armchair and sighed. 'I don't suppose Kiall will like it.'

Caroline looked at her incredulously. 'Who's that?'

'Obviously you've never been North before. Kiall Stirling is a descendant of one of our earliest settlers, a man who brought law and order to the wilds. The same qualities are fairly recognisable in Kiall. He won't take kindly to a child burying herself in the jungle. Especially not as you're Teddy Marshall's daughter. Your mother came out from England to marry his uncle.'

'But this is crazy!' Caroline shouted, quite frightened by all these revelations. 'My mother wasn't English!'

'My darling girl,' Miss Coddington said briskly to hide her own upset, 'I knew her well.'

'I think we'd better let the kid sit down,' Paddy said unhappily. It was a mistake for the girl to have come up here, he reflected. In the old days it had been a scandal the way Teddy had snatched that little angel from under Martin Stirling's nose.

'Did your father never tell you the story?' Miss Coddington asked, shocked.

'Frankly, all I can recall his saying to me was goodbye.'

Miss Coddington leant forward and covered Caroline's small hand with her own. 'I feared as much. Dear God, how he loved her! It was the most shattering blow when she . . . died. Do you remember anything at all about her?'

'How could I?' Caroline felt she was being attacked from all sides. 'She died when I was born.'

From Paddy came the most peculiar keening sound. 'That's the worst of being a little kid. No one will tell ya anything.'

'At any rate, not tonight.' Miss Coddington spoke firmly. '*Please* come back with me, Caroline. I wouldn't put it past Kiall to remove you forcibly when he hears of it.'

'He's got no authority whatever over me.' Caroline set her delicately determined jaw. 'All my life I've been told what to do. Now I'm going to hold on to my independence at all costs. To begin with, I have money—not a great deal, but enough. In just a couple of weeks from now I'll turn this place into a home.'

'Rah, rah! There's nothing wrong with *you*.' Miss Coddington gave her an approving glance. 'There's going to be hell to pay from Kiall, though. Dear God, you can't be . . . eighteen?' Swiftly she made the calculation.

'What's it got to do with him anyway?' Caroline demanded. Even the name had a devastating ring. Now that she came to think of it, the same name as the town.

'Everythin',' Paddy exclaimed succinctly. 'Mr Stirling is like a king to us simple country folks. If he doesn't want you out here on your own, you won't.'

'But that's intimidation!' Caroline blurted with a dangerous glint in her eye.

'It's only for ya own good.' Paddy looked down at her, deciding he liked her better now he could see she had a little fire. Although she was like enough to her exquisite little mother he was struck by the fact that she was far removed from a little angel. The same features as little Deborah, but from the look of it, the extreme opposite.

'Whoever persuaded you to come up here?' Joycie was asking, opening out all the windows.

'It seemed like a good idea at the time.'

At least she had a sense of humour, because Paddy saw the sombre mouth twitch. 'It was the house that made up my mind. I've never had anywhere to live in.'

'Don't, m'dear, I can't bear it.' Joyce Coddington was a woman of tremendous heart, and in less than an hour she had perceived what the child's life had been like. A tragedy, the whole business. Would anyone ever know the truth? 'You ought to have a telephone,' she said briskly.

'You think there's a chance Mr Stirling will let her stay?'

'What is he, some kind of monster?' Caroline stared at Paddy's intent face. 'I'm a grown-up person!'

'You only look a kid, if you want to know.'

'I'll look different when I get some make-up,' Caroline assured them.

'M'dear, it won't stay on you,' Miss Coddington told her, 'but you look perfectly beautiful without it. What you really want to discover is how to dress. None of those long slacks. I don't go around in these garments for nothing. It's impossible to constrict oneself in the heat. Fortunately I can take you out shopping.'

'Wouldn't she be better off with somebody else?' Paddy asked slyly, over his shoulder.

'There's nothing wrong with my taste,' Miss Coddington said serenely. 'When I was a gel I used to stop 'em in their tracks.'

'Ya still do!' Paddy told her with a roar of laughter. 'Now look, what are we gunna do about this little girl here?'

'I told you,' Caroline looked at them both severely. 'I'll be perfectly safe. There are locks on the doors . . . *are* there?'

Paddy glanced at Joyce and she nodded. 'The house is quite secure, though it might well topple over.'

'The white ants got to the stumps,' Paddy said gloomily. 'What's she gunna do for food?'

'We shall dispatch some groceries on the double.' Miss Coddington was chewing on her bottom lip looking at the girl's face. 'Much more to the point, how are you going to sleep? There are no bedclothes, no mosquito net. The last, m'dear, is an absolute essential. The mozzies here are as big as aircraft.'

Caroline's rare, enchanting smile suddenly appeared. 'To tell you the truth, all I thought of was getting here. You seem to understand, Miss Coddington.'

'*Joyce*, m'dear. Up here Miss Coddington sounds perfectly absurd.'

'Joyce,' Caroline said, not for a long time getting the easy hang of it. 'At least I've got a toothbrush.'

'You know damned well,' Paddy said irritably, 'Mr Stirling is not gunna like it. You're always so sensible, Joycie.'

'I can fathom the child's needs.' And though she could Joyce was still unhappy. Kiall could very well go into a blue rage. But what else could she do? It was apparent that the girl wasn't going to go with them. She was like a little creature of the wilds staking out its territory. 'Tomorrow,' she announced firmly, 'we can put things to order.'

'There are some pretty weird characters passin' through the North,' Paddy told her with the voice of long experience. 'A young girl's got no place bein' on her own.'

'I shall get a dog.' Caroline slapped at a flying insect.

'Gawd, you'd better get a dozen.' Paddy wondered unhappily if she knew how she looked. Not an angel, but a mermaid. If some young blade from the town called on her she'd be frightened out of her wits.

'A Dobermann would be the best,' Joyce considered, 'but not a favourite of mine. I could let you have Molly for the night.'

'*That* listless mutt?'

'Molly is an experienced watchdog,' Joyce said promptly.

'God knows, Joycie, ya need her yaself.' Paddy was back to cawing.

'I promise you both, I'll be quite all right.' It seemed necessary to reassure them both and Caroline spoke in Sister Bonaventure's strong, significant tones. The Almighty would take care of all.

It was another fifteen minutes before they would go; Paddy lapsing into recriminations that trailed off, Joyce chewing on her nether lip. Neither was happy.

They really care about me, Caroline thought in astonishment when no one except the nuns had ever cared what became of her. Sister Lucy had made her swear on the Blessed Mother that she would write, and that showed faith when Caroline wasn't even a Catholic.

The moment she was alone she went through to the largest bedroom and opened up her case. What items of clothing she had, she flung up in the air in disgust. Most of them she had made herself on Sister Lucy's machine.

'Terrific!' she cried aloud. 'Simply terrific!' She would go shopping all right and not finish up looking like Joycie, swathed about in an old curtain.

A cold shower gave her the greatest pleasure she had ever known. The water was beautifully soft and she poured shampoo on her hair luxuriating in the freedom from heat. A late afternoon breeze had sprung up and outside the uncovered window of the bathroom a great lavender-blue truss of a jacaranda sighed against the pane.

So much to be done! Now that she was cool, her spirits were soaring again and a secret smile curved her mouth. A home of her own. She would never give the place up. Still her triumph was edged with a bitter sadness. 'This was my father's home,' she said aloud, her voice echoing oddly. 'My father. The man I've never known!'

The mirror was badly speckled and she leaned closer to study her reflection. Already her hair was drying in a satin slide and it seemed to her she looked different. Her mouth wasn't set in the old way and there was a dreamy look in her slanted green eyes.

'He needn't think he'll get rid of me!' She tossed her long mane over her shoulder, thinking now she had pulled the arms out of her yellow cotton dress it looked just the thing. 'Now I'm here, I won't budge.'

Barefooted, she padded through the silent house. Doubtless she could transform it. New curtains, new slip covers, a lot of paint, and she saw a home. The view from every window was beautiful, the luxuriant blossoming growth, and the central core of the house was quite cool.

The dining room suite was surprisingly good, together with the Victorian sideboard. Caroline trailed a hand over the smooth mahogany of the table feeling a burst of pleasure. The wood was a beautiful colour and it would get lots of polishing. The redecorating of the house provided the most wonderful challenge. She just *knew* she could cope.

An hour later when Paddy returned with carton after carton of precious groceries he found her working; so busy and interested, for the first time he could see the person she was meant to be.

'Oh, Paddy, you're a darling!'

Even her voice sounded different—not the clipped young lady, but full of sunshine. He found himself beaming back.

'My word, you've made a difference!' He put the last carton down on the kitchen table and looked around him. 'You'll have to shut those windows, love.

The mozzies won't bother to have to take ya outside to eat ya.'

She almost ran to do as he asked, her cool, aloof manner gone. 'What am I going to do for air?'

'Don't worry, love, we'll get ya some screens up. Joycie has sent ya some bed things over, and a mosquito net. You've got a ring set up. I had a look.'

'Hey,' she said to him, 'you're a couple of friends.'

'By gee,' he turned to her, 'I'd think a girl like you would have scores of them.'

'No, Paddy.' Caroline shook her head. 'Sister Lucy called it my pride.'

'Oh well,' said Paddy. 'You'll make plenty up 'ere. What's really worryin' me is what Mr Stirling will say.'

She tilted her little chin. 'Why do you worry about him so much?'

'Lookin' after people is his business,' Paddy exclaimed. 'You might say he owns the town.'

'Everything?' Caroline felt a quiver of rage.

'You'll learn.' Paddy patted her shoulder comfortingly. 'Don't worry, love. He's a great bloke. The best. But don't go around tryin' to cross him. You'll strike trouble.'

Caroline raised her delicate brows. 'Perhaps he might do well not to cross *me*.'

'That's it, Teddy's girl!' Patting her shoulder more vigorously, Paddy propelled her towards the verandah, all the while telling her how to close up. The utility bucked under his hands, and only then did she think to lean in the window.

'But, Paddy, how much do I owe you?' With all her meals hitherto provided for her the thought of money had almost gone out of her mind.

'Another one of those beaut smiles.' Paddy looked

up to grin. 'Think of it as an 'ousewarmin', a gift from your friends.'

It was lucky he took off so quickly, for tears stung her eyes.

Friends. She had *friends*!

The brief mauve dusk was almost over. She hurried up the rickety steps and fortunately missed the snake that was curled somnolently beneath the rotting wood. Layers of her deep reserve were dropping from her like a burden. She had a future. Youth and hope. There was nothing that was not within her power.

It wasn't until a few hours later that she found it was all a matter of degree. Spirit she had in good measure, but there were some people impossible to take on.

CHAPTER THREE

So much activity had caused Caroline to have another shower, but by nine o'clock she was ready for bed. Joycie's cotton sheets smelt deliciously, not of lavender, but as she came to find out later, of boronia. Clouds of lemon mosquito netting enclosed her bed and once that was done, she opened wide the windows. At least when she was safely inside they wouldn't get her, and the night air was cool and blissfully fragrant.

She paused for two minutes to say her prayers then went back into the kitchen to turn the light on. Of course it would shoot up her electricity bill, but she had to have some glimmer of light, at least until she got used to her new surroundings. A night light would be best. She would get one in the morning. And a car. A car first, then the licence. She would teach herself on the back tracks.

Almost in darkness, the house didn't seem quite so welcoming. It was pitch black outside and there were lots of rustlings and scurryings from the trees. She knew as well as anyone else it was probably possums, but she was beginning to feel a teeny bit nervous. How silly!

A minute or so later when something dropped on the roof, she told herself aloud it was a fruit bat who just missed out on a mango. As she was going to stay here by herself it would be handy to have a stockpile of useful little excuses. She had never, ever, been nervous at the convent even when some silly halfwit had spent a brisk half hour shinning up a drainpipe that led to the girl's dormitories. Sister Bonaventure had been waiting and had treated him to a swipe that sent him spinning back to a waiting police car.

There, she felt better already! One had only to think of Sister Bonaventure to rise above any situation. She smiled at herself in the speckled hallway mirror, then swung around in shock as headlights threw up across the front verandah.

Oh, hell! she thought resentfully, trembling with the full force of a woman's intuition, it's that lovable old tyrant, Kiall Stirling. Paddy had been certain he would come. He might even have suggested it, that being a man's way. Men really had no opinion of women. The very few she had met had given her that strong impression. Now she was about to meet the resident dictator in her sweet little housecoat and bare feet.

The thump on the door was impressive—a sure sign of his disposition.

'Miss Marshall?'

Caroline found herself glowering at the tone. Big voice, big man, or at any rate—bulk.

Specifically to annoy him she called out in a quivery, little nervous voice: 'Who's there?'

'Kiall Stirling.' He said it as though that said everything.

She never even knew she possessed an impish sense of humour. 'But I don't know you.'

'You will if you open up the door,' he responded dryly.

'But I can't!' she called with feigned terror. 'How do I even know you're who you say?' She was longing for the next exchange.

'What in God's name do you want—a driver's licence?'

He was a little angry, she could tell. 'That, or a credit card.'

'In any case,' he said insolently, 'I have a key.'

The little girl nervousness dropped from her tone, betraying her true character. 'After you shove it under the door, why don't you drop back tomorrow?'

An instant's silence, then a clear: 'Cut out the horse-play and open the door.'

Steely as she felt Caroline realised it was better to do as he asked. He seemed a singularly unpleasant and obstinate beast. She flicked her long hair behind her back and threw open the door, falling back in genuine terror as a tall, dark-haired man confronted her.

'It can't be!' Even her lips lost colour.

'For God's sake!' She was retreating from him step by step and he caught her shoulders and held her upright. 'If I were Dracula I could understand!'

Her green eyes were frozen and one small hand sought to shield her averted face. On no account would she ever be left alone again. 'Who are you?' she asked hoarsely, and to her horror began to weep.

He was staring at her incredulously, then when it became apparent that there was going to be no let-up to her anguish he swung her disgustedly off her feet.

'Take it easy,' he said grimly. 'I've frightened you. I'm sorry.'

Her agitation was so intense she was trembling all over her slight frame. On the old sofa she still kept her face averted, half hidden in the musty cushions, and the sight of her caused his white teeth to snap together.

'You aren't in the slightest danger,' he said caustically, 'though clearly if you keep this up you'll finish in a lunatic asylum.'

'God help me!' Caroline confirmed it, and took a shuddering breath.

'Am I that terrifying?' he asked harshly, and turned her smothered face to him forcibly.

'At least you're here in body as well as spirit!' She gave an hysterical little cry.

'What the hell——' He looked angry and bewildered. 'Are you totally out of control?'

Now that he held her chin, she couldn't keep from staring. The same face as in her locket. She was as fascinated as she was terror-stricken. 'You're *dead*,' she announced.

'And you're crazy! Or sick.' The biting sarcasm gave way to concern and he touched a hand to her brow.

'The nuns always told me the soul was immortal.'

'And you've awakened to the dreadful day?' He was staring at her with a clinical intensity. 'You have no temperature at all.' Against the forest green of the cushions, her hair looked more silver than gold, young skin like a pearl, outsize frightened eyes.

'Am I about to encounter the other world?' she asked.

'For what my opinion's worth to you,' he said acidly, 'I'd say, *no*. If you can settle down and just talk to me, maybe you can tell me why you're nearly dying of fright?'

Let me hold on to my sanity! she prayed. 'Who *are* you?'

'Dear God!' He hit his forehead in exasperation. 'All right, we'll start again. My name, orphan Annie, is Kiall Stirling. It may be your habit to visualise the worst, but your appearance is against you. At best you look a child, at worst, vaguely demented.'

'But then that's because you look like my father!'

'The hell I do!' he exclaimed with positive brutality.

'But I'd know your face anywhere.' The tears fell from her eyes.

'Really?' His expression had become detestable. 'Come to that, I'd know *you*!'

Caroline wouldn't have been surprised if flames had burst from his feet. Maybe he was the devil or she'd gone troppo like Salvo. Not yet! 'If you go into my bedroom, you'll find a gold locket,' she said valiantly. 'Bring it out.' Hadn't Paddy said the house was haunted?

He gave her a glance that said 'brain damage' and stood up. To make it worse, it was still young. Thirty-three or four as he had been, stayed exactly, as in the faded little photo. His shoulders were very wide, his waist and hips very lean. He had the most striking kind of colouring there was; jet black hair and light eyes, gleaming dark copper skin.

Close encounters of the other kind. She tried to straighten up on the sofa, but her limbs had gone fluid. It was enough to turn anyone's mind. Her mother's property had been given to her by Mr Randall on her fourteenth birthday. A few modest pieces of jewellery, among them a distinctly Victorian locket, heart-shaped and set with semi-precious stones. Inside were the two faces she had talked to all the time: her mother and father.

He moved back across the room to her and sat down on the sofa near her vulnerable, small feet.

'Well?' He held the locket out to her.

It was swinging gently and she stared at it for some moments. 'Open it.'

'As you lack the energy,' He sprang the catch and as he looked down at what was inside, his handsome face was filled with a hard light. 'The lovers,' he said harshly.

'My mother and father.'

'Who the devil told you that?'

'I'm not frightened,' Caroline murmured, when she felt he would slap her. In that respect he looked violent.

'You really know how to torture.' He almost flung the locket at her so it slipped from her breast to her lap. 'That man is my uncle Martin. He was *not* your father. He might well have been, only your foolish little mother threw him off in the most peculiar fashion. A woman's nature. It appears you take after her—not only to look at.'

She shook with even more violence. 'Your *Uncle Martin*?'

'The cushions match your eyes.' The handsome mouth thinned. 'Who told you any different? Let me guess. Your poor demented father. Infidelity sent him crazy.'

'*Stop!*' She grasped his arm and instantly felt the shock.

'You started it, Goldie, with the fey act. Have you come up to claim that you're my little cousin?'

'And who's to say I'm not?' She felt nerveless with shock. Those two people in her locket had loved each other; she knew that with certainty.

'So *that's* it!' He stood up so quickly he nearly toppled her to the floor. 'Some actress! Paddy told me about this spunky little kid, but he forgot to mention that she was a budding little con-woman.'

He couldn't humiliate her. She wasn't even listening. His Uncle Martin. For years now she had been wrong. Or had she? She wouldn't rest until she knew.

'I want to see him—your uncle.' Her green eyes were enormous.

The winged brows drew together and for an instant he looked explosive. 'How old are you?' He was no longer looking at her as if she were a child, but a paid actress.

'Seventeen.' Her housecoat was above her knees and she settled it abstractedly.

'And your father's dead?'

'Edward Marshall is.'

'Say that again and I'll slap you!'

Caroline didn't deceive herself that he wouldn't do it. He was a very handsome man but as hard as nails. 'I always believed the two people in my locket were my mother and father.'

'Ah!' he murmured with a frightening dryness. 'And how did you come by this locket?'

She sat up slowly and tucked her feet neatly under her. 'Mr Randall gave me my mother's things on my fourteenth birthday.'

'When you decided Martin Stirling was your father?'

'Why would I think otherwise?'

'You have great promise as an actress,' he told her.

'You don't believe me?' She sighed heavily and let her gaze travel over his face.

'Or someone's taught you well.'

'I don't think you know how I've suffered.'

His silver eyes sparkled in the light. 'So now you've come up here to put things right?'

'I've come because for the first time in my life I have a home.'

'Bravo!' He put his hands together with bitter humour. 'You've got it all together beautifully. Can't you just go away?'

'But I want to stay!' Caroline sat up swiftly and swayed.

'Forget the pose, honey—and it *is* a pose.' The sparkling eyes slashed over her. 'So life's hard for a little orphan, how much do you want?'

'Everything, I guess.' She couldn't shake the eerie feelings that beset her.

He shook his head. 'You talk big.'

'Where is this uncle of yours?' she demanded.

His speed was dazzling, for he lifted her up from the sofa and gave her a painful shake. The dark face looked primitive, even savage. 'Don't play games with me, you'll get hurt!'

'Where *is* he?' she shouted.

'I won't have you come here and start trouble.'

'Damn it, I have a right to live!'

'So did Martin!' His eyes were filled with a relentless anger.

All at once it came to her and she slumped under his steely hands. 'He's dead?'

There was danger in the room, violence, but she disregarded it in the search for truth. 'If you were a young man I'd thrash you,' he said tautly.

'There's *nothing* you can do to me.'

'A damned lot, I'd say.' He dropped a hard hand beneath her chin.

'You wouldn't hurt me?' She gave a stifled little moan, confused by the wild emotions that raged in her own breast.

'I will if you don't run.'

He was hurting her, but she dared not put up her hand. It was peculiar to be so close to this man and her young face went very pale.

'Frightened at last?' He let her go abruptly, staring down at her with a look of terrible arrogance. 'You little fool, in coming up here you've exposed yourself to risk.'

'But how? Please tell me.' She fell down again, on to the sofa.

'Plenty of people remember your mother. The way she humiliated our family and finally brought us tragedy.'

'I can see that in your face.' Caroline bent her head so her hair fell around her in a shining curtain. 'I can't go away. Don't you see, I have no place to go.'

'Then I'll write you a cheque as soon as you like.' His silver eyes glittered with an unnatural brilliance and he regarded her with a mixture of disgust and pity. 'You're so young, but then she was young too. I remember her.'

'You're so cruel!' she exclaimed.

'And you're not even eighteen. Only you've picked the wrong man.'

'Have I?' She lifted her head and stared up at him, beauty for all the torment.

'For a kid you've got high ambitions.' The sardonic voice was full of contempt.

'I've had *nothing* all my life!'

'So now's the right moment for the big change.' The contempt was searing, but she still paid no attention. Her nerves were screaming. There were too many secrets to her past, too many mysteries to unravel. At that moment, she could cope with no more.

As he watched her sitting there so dazedly, his hostility seemed to thaw a little, not a softening, but an involuntary sympathy for her youth, the physical defencelessness. He laughed a little, with no humour to the sound.

'If you'll get a few things together, I'll take you back to Maralaya.'

She recovered a little and shook her loose hair. 'It's peace I want.'

'Little imbecile!'

'So I'll stay here. This is the house Edward Marshall left me.'

'So who else did he have? He was always a loner.'

She stared over his jet black head at the blazing light bulb. 'Maybe I know now why he never wanted me.'

'For instance, you must have reminded him of Deborah. She pretended to be so angelic, but she wasn't angelic at all.'

'Who *is*?' she said simply. 'I've never met one in my life.' There was a faint colour now in her pale lips, not full, but exquisite in their chiselling. 'You hate me, don't you?'

'Because you've seen an opportunity?' His dark face was inscrutable.

'You don't know!' she exclaimed wildly.

'*Don't* I?' He stared at her tragic face indifferently. 'For God's sake, your father was a snake.'

'Prove to me that your uncle wasn't!'

Her passionate challenge hit home. He moved away from her restlessly, keeping his temper under control.

'What is it you're really after—money? Or to deliberately stir up trouble?'

'Neither.' She drew her simple flowered housecoat around her with dignity. 'I want to find out who I am.'

'You're Ted Marshall's child, and nobody else's.'

She swallowed sharply. 'Do I look like him?'

A muscle jumped in his temple. Her face was still raised, her hair shining in the harsh light. 'You look like Deborah, the little English girl who touched all our hearts. I was only fourteen at the time, but she got to me as well. She was good at it.'

'She was very pretty.' Caroline bent over her locket again.

'Beautiful, like in a Greek tragedy. And that's exactly how it was.'

'*Tell* me.' Her voice sounded young and agonised.

'You don't know?' His voice sounded positive she was lying.

'I never saw the man I believed to be my father after I was eight. He never spoke to me of anything. He put me in a boarding school, and left me.'

'And you don't remember what he looked like?' Again the disbelief.

'I thought—the same as in the photo. He was tall and dark—handsome.'

'Ted was a good-looking man.' His face darkened. 'I suppose in type he shared a similarity with my uncle. The important thing is, you can't stay on.'

'Oh, I will,' she said wearily, and met his shimmering eyes. 'Because *you* don't want me here is simply not enough.'

'Once the town sees you, knows you're here, there's bound to be a reaction.'

'Two of them are my friends.' It seemed like a miracle to be able to say it.

'Remember I told you, Deborah drew them in.'

'You're over-reacting.'

'There's nothing I won't do to stop you causing trouble.' His deep voice went harsh. 'If you thought this trip was going to be profitable, then, if you insist, it will be. The conditions are, however, you pack up and go back to where you belong.'

'They don't want me back again at the convent.' Caroline tilted her head regally.

'What convent?' Kiall Stirling asked thoughtfully.

She raised her delicate brows. 'So you can check?'

'I'll be damned if I'll go along with your entire story!'

'If it wasn't so ludicrous,' she said distinctly, 'I'd say you were frightened of me.'

'Okay,' his mouth thinned in mockery, 'let's say for the sake of argument I *am* frightened of a little bitty con-woman?'

'You're frightened of what I'll uncover.'

'Okay—shoot. Everyone knows the story, including you. Poor old Teddy couldn't have carried that one around with him. We couldn't shut him up years ago.'

'Why don't you go away?' she said in a small, bewildered voice. 'I feel sick.'

'Nothing quite as neat as you intended?'

'Anyway, this is my house.'

'Why don't you go into town tomorrow and start crying rape?' he drawled.

Oh, the insult! Her eyes were ablaze with it. How dared he come here with his wickedness! She gathered herself together in one lunge, twisting up her hand, hitting him and revelling in the smarting.

'Don't you think for one instant you can intimidate *me*!' Anger overrode every last bit of caution.

'And don't *you* think you can throw punches at *me*!' His reaction was instantaneous. Another minute she was across his knee making plaintive noises. 'I should have done this earlier.'

He didn't even pick her up when she slid with astonishment on to the floor. 'You're a savage!' He looked like one with his black, smouldering looks.

'You look flushed.' He looked at her with a rueful, mocking smile.

'What do you do next? Throw me into the snake-pit?'

'Don't worry, I'll think up all sorts of things.' The disturbing smile was gone. 'Now, if you've subsided there's nothing else to be done but to take you home.'

'Is this the way you always treat newcomers?' His silver eyes had narrowed and the handsome mouth had a hint of cruelty.

'You can't stay here. I don't want you.'

She moved up from the floor in a naturally graceful balletic flow. 'You don't seem to understand. In spite of your opposition I'm staying!'

He caught her hand and pulled her to him. 'Go away before I hurt you.'

'Hurt me? How?'

'You're terrific, really,' he said. 'A terrific actress. Big green eyes and a look of absolute innocence.'

'You're very like your uncle, aren't you?' she answered, appraising him as he was appraising her.

'Don't delude yourself, Goldie,' he told her with severity. 'There's not a woman alive I couldn't shake off.'

'You're not married?' Why wouldn't he let go of her hand? The sensation of skin on skin was peculiar.

'I don't even play around.'

'I shouldn't think so.' With an effort she jerked her hand away. 'You haven't got the face for it.'

'A monster.' He gave that disturbingly attractive smile again and she wished he wouldn't. 'Well?' he said.

'Well *what*?'

'My car's outside.'

'I'll walk you to it.' Anything to get rid of him.

His agreement took her by surprise. 'Aren't you frightened of walking about in bare feet?'

'All right, I'll get my slippers.'

'Good girl.' He seemed to be pleased with her. How curious!

When Caroline stepped out on to the verandah, she nearly went crazy shrieking. '*Yoicks!*' A grimace of violent distaste contorted her pearly face.

'Don't mind them, my dear.' He put out a long arm and jerked her to his side. 'Just a few cane toads.'

'But they're tremendous!'

They were. They were atrocious!

'Little fellers really. You should see some of the savages.'

'My God!' Caroline's voice was quavery with shock. 'Do they get into the house?' she asked him.

'Don't be surprised if you find one in your bath.'

His car wasn't Paddy's little job but a huge station wagon. 'Thanks for worrying about me anyway,' she said acidly.

'I can see you're not the type that goes running scared.'

'Not me!' She felt absurdly pleased.

Caroline had a moment of looking up at the brilliant stars, then she was crushed dazedly against him. 'In you go.'

Could this possibly be a kidnapping? Certainly it seemed like it. 'Let me go!'

'That's impossible, honey.' He shoved her casually through the door.

'You can't expect me to take this lying down!' She was positively bellowing because she was so very angry, but in the end she had to stop because her mouth seemed to be full of mosquitoes. She spat them out with an awful impulse to cry.

'Settle back.' Kiall flicked a switch and the air conditioning came on, blowing over the idling sound of the engine.

'You may remember that kidnapping is a criminal offence.'

'Rubbish,' he said crisply. 'You're my little house guest.'

'The front door is wide open.'

'Don't worry,' he glanced at her briefly and she shivered, 'no one will come near it. The place has been abandoned.'

'Like me.' That was how she generally thought of herself. Abandoned. The girl child no one had ever wanted. 'I haven't even got a toothbrush!'

'What a damn nuisance,' he drawled.

CHAPTER FOUR

MARALAYA, a handful of miles away, was the ultimate in a tropical mansion, with distinct echoes of the American Deep South.

In the daytime it was paradise with the sun on the majestic grounds and gardens, now the house was like a great ship at night.

'Did you build it yourself?' Light spilled from this aristocratic residence that seemed to extend across a hilltop commanding sweeping views of the workers toiling in the canefields.

'Not exactly.' His dry voice had a catch of humour. 'In this part of the world, this is an historic house, a little whimsy my great-grandfather thought up.'

'Very dramatic!'

'It's good for entertaining,' he pointed out.

'Not the house for dogs and boots and muddy shoes?'

'Or a pint sized silver-blonde in a floral housecoat. Where did you get it, by the way? Lifeline?'

'I made it,' she said tartly. 'We're not all filthy with money.'

'Your only assets are youth and beauty?'

'I have a house in the country and a few thousand dollars.'

'You'll have to spend them, otherwise your house in the country is going to fall down.'

'By the time I'm finished with it,' she said smartly, 'it'll be beautiful!'

'For a little poker face that had a certain ring of

passion,' observed Kiall dryly.

'Kindly look at yourself!'

'Be careful with that tongue,' he warned.

'I hope you live alone?' she said wretchedly, leaning forward to get a better view of the house.

'I'm sorry, how's that again?' The silver eyes swept over her.

'I'm not a little girl, you know,' she pointed out severely. 'I've got no damned clothes on, none to put on, and you've placed me in a very embarrassing position.'

'We'll go in the back way.'

'I'm old-fashioned, I'd like to go in the front.' Don't push me through the servants' entrance, she thought wrathfully. She might have been wearing a housecoat, but many a person could mistake it for a perfectly good dress.

Just outside the entrance hall her mouth nearly dropped open. It was just like the Archbishop's, hung with crystal and Old Masters and the richness of elaborate plasterwork. A monumental staircase dominated her eye and she had a vivid picture of herself wafting down the Persian carpet in the most gorgeous, opulent ball gown. It was definitely a Scarlett O'Hara landscape. Another world.

A voice sounded from the upper gallery, calling out in sharp tones: 'Who's there?'

'I'd like to go home, please.' Caroline turned on her captor.

'Why, don't you like it?' he asked.

'Perhaps I do, and perhaps I don't. In any case, I have a home of my own.'

'And I'll take you back to it when the sun's out.' Gently but very firmly Kially propelled her through the great red cedar double doors.

A woman stood on the landing of the staircase, a handsome, stern-faced woman as conventionally dressed as Miss Coddington had been outlandish.

Caroline knew instantly which one she liked.

'Why, Kiall——' She came down the stairs, glancing briefly at Kiall Stirling, then subjecting Caroline to a piercing regard. Her resemblance to Kiall Stirling was unmistakable, but whereas the family looks were breathtaking in the male, they were too strong and decisive in the female. Both had stunning self-assurance, but it was apparent the woman, in her late fifties, was experiencing some shock.

The lancing grey eyes levelled on Caroline as though they could never look away. 'Who *are* you?' the woman drawled.

Caroline felt acutely disturbed and tried to erase the feeling by acting cool.

'I'm Caroline Marshall.'

'Don't you dare come in here!'

Caroline stiffened and she felt the hot blood whip into her cheeks. 'As a matter of fact, it was your son who took the notion into his head to kidnap me,' she retorted.

'Kiall!' the woman put out a hand to him and Caroline saw to her bewilderment that it was trembling. 'Who is she? Where has she come from?'

'Hush, Thea,' he said, and there seemed to be some kind of intent, some warning, in his voice. 'She's who she says she is—Ted Marshall's daughter.'

'That scoundrel!'

'Are you finished?' Caroline asked politely. 'I told your son bringing me here was a wild idea. Not mine, I assure you.'

'At least she doesn't talk like *her*.' The grey eyes were as cold and forbidding as an Arctic winter.

'Don't you want to find out how I came to be here?'
Caroline jutted her small chin. The father a scoundrel.
The mother a *her*.

'Let's go inside and shut the door,' Kiall Stirling
said firmly.

'*You* shut the door,' Caroline told him tartly. 'I'm
on my way back to the farm.'

'The farm?' The woman called Thea froze in her
tracks. 'You're not living there?'

'I intend to, madam.' Not for nothing had Caroline
had a lifetime of living with the nuns. She didn't know
it, but she had Mother Superior and Sister Bonaventure off to a T.

The tone was enough even to quiet this hostile
woman. 'What are we to *do*, Kiall?' she wailed.

'Put the child to bed. She's all eyes.'

'Green eyes,' the woman said bitterly. 'I feel extremely ill.'

'Forgive me.' Caroline tried to soften her tone with
some of Mother Superior's forbearance. 'I can see
you're upset, Mrs Stirling, but it's not clear to me why.
I understand I look like my mother, but is that so un-
forgivable?'

The woman stared at her, not answering, and as
Caroline put out an appealing hand, she flung herself
away.

'You must leave here at once.'

'I'd do so if your son would stop playing the heavy
and open the door.'

'He's *not* my son,' the woman burst out explosively.
'Kiall is my nephew, my brother's son. This is my
home.'

'What you don't seem to understand,' Caroline said
wearily, 'is that I *want* to go.'

'I will *not* have all the old tragedies resurrected

again!' The woman wrung her hands in anguish and no matter what else Caroline thought, she could see that her upset was genuine.

'Perhaps it would be better, Thea, if we talked this thing over privately.' Kiall Stirling put his hand on his aunt's shoulder. 'I want no more of this than you do, but she's here now.'

Caroline's eyes flashed to his dark face. 'Didn't anyone teach you not to speak about people as though they're not there?'

'Do you want another slap?'

Thea Stirling looked from one to the other with the strained look of one who is suffering a painful memory, then she turned away completely and disappeared into the shining drawing room.

'Now I know what it truly means to be a ghoul.'

'Ghost,' he corrected her, though it was obvious his thoughts were dark. 'If you'll come upstairs I'll show you where you can sleep?'

'Why not a cupboard? Isn't that where ghosts clank their chains?' She was so miserable she could have cried, but crying had been drilled out of her. Instead of going to pieces she resorted to her usual, slightly bitter flippancy. 'Who are you, after all, to keep me here against my will?'

'Oh, shut up!' He nearly thrust her up the stairs.

The gallery was hung about with paintings with here and there an antique chair. 'What did you do to make all this money? Kill a Chinaman?'

'They weren't the only ones to make it in the big gold rushes. Actually my family were what was known as swells.'

'How lovely!' She preceded him into a gigantic bed-room, which could have accommodated a skating rink. 'Only a swell could talk thus.'

'Isn't it time you stopped being flip?' he said coldly.

Caroline gave a choked sound. 'Close your ears if you don't want to hear me. Close your eyes.'

His hand on her delicate shoulder was rough. 'All right, settle down.'

'As you please, milord.' She took a flying leap on to the bed. 'If you don't go away, I'll start to undress.'

'That will give me something to laugh about.' He ignored her and went to the pairs of French doors, opening them out. After that he slid the insect screens into place. 'There's a bathroom through the adjoining door. I'll get Hilda to find you some clothes for the morning.'

'And who, pray, is Hilda? The old family retainer?'

'I suppose you have to say *something*.'

She sat up in the huge fourposter bed and stared at him. 'You're a hard man, but I think you're trying to be kind to me.'

'Maybe I just think you're more wronged against than wronging.' His glance, striking her face and her body made her give a soft shiver.

'Perhaps I'd better stay awake.' Now why had she said that? Why would she even want to say it?

'You're a provoking little witch, and undoubtedly cunning,' Kiall told her.

'I shall lock the door.'

'Your face is wrong too. I've got a long memory.'

That night Caroline had a series of nightmares. One was so vivid, so distressing, she sat up in bed in fright.

Where the devil am I? For an instant she really couldn't remember then all the grim details came rushing back. The room was flooded with moonlight, an enchanting fragrance from the garden, but still she turned on the bedside lamp. A small porcelain clock showed three o'clock.

Her dreams had been eerie, crowded with faces—the two faces in her locket, a formless stranger, Paddy and Joyce had been there and the young solicitor, Ian Randall. He had been telling her something . . . something . . . something frightful, She couldn't remember.

In the glimmering light, the big bedroom was very beautiful, a place of peace and seclusion and obviously very feminine, the blossom-strewn wallpaper copied again in the two armchairs and the sofa, the silk taffeta fabric that made up the gorgeous quilt. She could see herself reflected in the Venetian mirror above an inlaid ebony chest of drawers. In a room of such proportions, she looked very small.

'What *is* it that I must find out?'

The girl in the mirror didn't answer her. There was so much that was hidden.

She slept fitfully after that, and when she finally opened her eyes she saw a small, plump woman in a neat button-through sort of uniform drawing back the insect screens.

'Good morning.'

Thank God! A friendly voice.

'Good morning.' Caroline found herself smiling sweetly. 'I'm sorry——' she glanced hurriedly at the clock, 'I seem to have slept late.'

'Of course, dear, but that's to be expected. You've done a bit of travelling.'

'Breakfast in bed?' Caroline protested, her eye for the first time falling on the laden tray.

'Mr Kiall ordered it especially.' The woman smiled fondly, her plump cheeks rosy—no doubt from the morning bake.

'You're Hilda, aren't you?' said Caroline.

'Yes, miss.' Hilda settled the tray across Caroline's

knees. It was beautifully set with the best silver and bone china, a dew-touched pink rose bud, yet irresistibly a few lines from a Danny Kaye re-run sprang to Caroline's mind:

The pellet with the poison's in the chalice from the palace.

Should I drink?

Fortunately Hilda, who had prepared the morning brew, was unaware of Caroline's misgivings. 'Hope you like pineapple juice, miss? I've just put it through the processor.'

'Lovely!' Caroline felt ashamed of her train of thought.

'As for the rest of it, Mr Kiall was sure you'd like ham and eggs.'

'He's a wonderful man!' Caroline said dryly.

Hilda didn't hear the irony. 'The best boss I've ever had.'

If I don't indulge in a little gossip I'll find out nothing, Caroline thought. 'Have you been here long, Hilda?'

'Just on four years.' Hilda smiled and her bright blue eyes crinkled. 'A bed of roses after my last job. He was a millionaire too, but so mean!'

'Cursed, lucky thing!'

'Pardon, miss?'

'Mr Kiall's aunt is a charming woman.' What a way to put it!

Hilda's eyes lost their crinkle. 'She's very fair, but of course it's Mr Kiall's house. I respect him for looking after his maiden aunt.'

Caroline raised her eyebrows. *Miss* Stirling, but unlike Joycie, she would wager, not by choice. One could scarcely grieve for the ones that got away.

'And Mr Kiall's parents?' she asked.

'You don't know them, miss?' Hilda stooped to pick up a bit of fluff from the carpet.

'The Stirlings? No.'

'But his father is dead, miss. It was in all the papers—a business trip to New Guinea, and the plane went down. Plunged right into a mountain. No one around here cares to remember it. The whole North went into mourning. Why, Mrs Stirling, Mr Kiall's mother, couldn't live here any more. She's in England now with a married daughter.'

Caroline put her empty glass of pineapple juice down and sank back against the pillows. 'I must say I'm surprised,' she commented.

'But I thought. . . .' Hilda looked embarrassed.

'That I was a friend of theirs?'

'Aren't you, miss?'

'Actually I think it has something to do with child welfare.' She smiled at Hilda kindly. 'The pineapple juice was delicious.'

'From our own plantation,' Hilda said reverently. 'With respect, miss, you'd better eat up your ham and eggs or it will get cold.'

'Yes, I will.' Caroline studied her plate gravely. The thought of a big breakfast didn't lie easily on her unsettled stomach, but it was one of the better aspects of her character that she accepted the good with the bad. 'Thank you, Hilda.'

Hilda returned the smile and prepared to go. 'By the way, miss, I've left some clothes in your wardrobe.'

'Where did you happen to get them?' Caroline looked towards the wardrobe door.

'There's plenty, miss. Miss Nina, Mr Kiall's sister, leaves a complete wardrobe.'

'Meaning she's some place else?'

'Greece, miss. She loves it. She's not coming home

for another year.'

Caroline just stopped herself from asking some more questions. So he had a mother, two sisters, perhaps more? She would make it her business to chat Hilda up again.

Despite the nightmarish excesses of the night, she was able to tuck the big breakfast away. The croissants were superb. The only time the boarders had ever been allowed to eat them was on Bastille Day. The thought of her higher education made her pleat her brow. She had been such a good student. Sevens all the way.

Now to get dressed! Depressing thought. There would be Miss Stirling to avoid. When she opened up the wardrobe she fell back in spontaneous pleasure. The Stirling standards were very high, for the absent Nina dressed in silk. Caroline stared at one dress, then another; fingered the material. No wonder Kiall hadn't been taken by her housecoat!

A bit wistfully she shut the wardrobe door. One could get hooked on taking charity and she had always had her pride. She would just have to wander home in her housecoat and take great care never to get caught again.

Fighting down her feelings of embarrassment and confusion, she later found her way downstairs. There were voices coming from one of the front rooms.

'Don't worry, Thea, Kiall will get it all sorted out.' A good voice, a bit nasal.

'How can I *not* worry?' Miss Stirling, sounding funny-peculiar. 'I tell you the girl's here to make trouble. She's the very image of Deborah.'

'Then she's pretty?' This, with undisguised flatness.

'More. She's one of those women who only bring distress.'

A sexpot! Can they possibly be talking about *me*?

Caroline thought weakly. The most standoffish girl in the whole school. She felt furiously angry and affronted. Poor Miss Stirling's fears were based on an utterly false premise. She wasn't her captivating little mother at all. She was a serious, even stern person, intellectually above throwing men off balance.

So what do I do now? The lonely years had developed the ingrained habit of talking to herself. At least she never allowed her lips to move; then people really would think she was unhinged. Could she run out of the front door? To where? It was all so ridiculous, and she loathed looking ridiculous.

'*Pride*, Caroline,' Sister Lucy used to say. 'You have it, you know—to a fault!'

But *was* it? How else could she have survived all those pitying eyes. Doesn't Marshall have a family?

For a moment she thought of Edward Marshall. Was it because he suspected he wasn't her father that he had deserted her? There had to be a good reason for a man to abandon his only child. Or perhaps he had another family in Africa. The possibilities were limitless.

Just as she was debating what to do, the owners of the female voices walked into the entrance hall. Both, looking up at her, appeared astonished.

'Good morning.' Caroline's reaction was spontaneous. One always said good morning, though often she had thought, why?

It was difficult to say who was the more surprised, Miss Stirling or her visitor—a young woman in her mid-twenties, tall, prodigiously slim, with an elegant cap of dark curls and bright blue eyes. She was very attractive, a sophisticated outdoor girl, with a gleaming golden skin.

She had no right to look so shocked, then openly disapproving.

'Good morning.' Miss Stirling's face was a study. 'I believe Hilda brought clothing to your room?'

Caroline could see it was a real effort for her to speak. 'Many thanks,' she said politely, 'but I have my own.'

'For goodness' sake!' the brunette contributed a cold laugh. 'Are you really Ted Marshall's daughter?'

'Of course she is!' Miss Stirling answered for Caroline. Violently.

The brunette was still standing transfixed and Caroline addressed the older woman.

'I wonder if someone might drive me back to the farm?'

'*I* will.' The brunette laughed a little harshly. 'You don't mean to tell me you're staying there?'

'Of course,' Caroline answered nonchalantly. 'After all, it belongs to me.'

The brunette laughed again, a contemptuous light in her blue eyes. 'I suppose you know it's haunted?'

'Rubbish!' Caroline retorted promptly. 'The haunting is in people's minds.'

Miss Stirling made a little sound of distress. 'I believe Kiall is coming back for you.'

'And so he should, as he brought me here in the first place.' Caroline was back to giving her tight-lipped imitations.

This precipitated another gale of laughter. 'I say, you're priceless!'

'And you're . . . .?' Caroline looked down her small, straight noise.

'Danae Edgeley.'

'A close family friend,' Miss Stirling tacked on, grim-eyed. 'I understand Hilda has given you breakfast. If you're ready, Danae will take you home. So kind of you, Danae!' She turned to the younger woman, who placed a consoling hand on her arm.

'No bother at all, Thea. Anything to help.'

Like a stray puppy to the pound! Did none of these people allow a person dignity?

'I'm thinking of bringing charges against Mr Stirling,' Caroline announced, pretending anger. Why not?

Miss Stirling looked as though she was about to faint and even the arrogant Miss Edgeley looked nervous.

'I beg your pardon?'

'Kidnapping is a criminal offence,' Caroline explained.

'Don't be silly, you're having a good time.' Kiall Stirling chose that very moment to walk through the front door, flicking Caroline's slender frame with a look of unholy satire.

'Thanks for coming back for me,' she said caustically.

'I said I would.' His voice was flippant, but a sardonic little smile played about his sculptured mouth. 'Hi, Danae. I saw your car outside.'

'Thea rang me,' Danae told him.

'Really?' The silver eyes travelled from Danae to his silent aunt. 'Surely that wasn't necessary, Thea?'

'*I* thought so, dear,' Miss Stirling said in her precise, controlled voice. 'Danae is such a comfort to me, as you know.'

'Well, come along then, Caroline,' said Kiall dryly. 'It would seem you've rejected Nina's clothes.'

'I appreciate the offer,' she assured him, only at that minute coming on down the stairs.

'It's no trouble for me to drive her home,' Danae told him, her blue eyes afire. Her whole face, at the sight of him, had now become lyrical, softening in a way that told Caroline instantly: here was a girl in love!

'You're a friend in need, Danae,' he said smoothly,

'but I want to take another look at that farmhouse. It'll roll right over in the next blow.'

'Does that really matter?' she asked with undisguised astonishment. 'I mean, this child can't stay there. What will people say?'

Caroline very much resented the 'child' bit and beside Kiall Stirling she felt even more diminutive. 'Allow me to clear up one detail,' she told them all, 'I'm here and I'm going to stay.'

'Come along, Caroline.' Kiall Stirling took hold of her arm maddeningly.

'Do stop telling me what to do!' she snapped.

'Why do you automatically rebel about everything?' he asked dryly, looking down at her.

'Because I've been pushed around all my life.'

'I would have thought that would tend to make you quiet.' The dark, handsome face was very sardonic.

'May I come too?' Danae asked eagerly.

'Yes, go,' Miss Stirling agreed, obviously in a panic about something.

'Don't ask him, ask me.' Caroline turned her blonde head. 'It's my house!'

'Well then, dear,' Danae smiled sweetly, 'may I please see over it?'

'Take care!' Kiall murmured, before Caroline had time to answer.

'Really there's nothing to see.' Caroline was anything but a fool and she was following Danae's reasoning. 'But don't worry, give me a little time and I'll turn it into a showplace.'

'Good grief!' Danae's black eyebrows rose in simple disbelief. 'I'll come anyway.'

In the brilliant light of morning, the farm looked even more ramshackle.

'A jewel!' said Caroline, from the back seat. 'I was

quite good at art, I may take up painting!' Threatened on all sides, she had spirit in good measure.

'God, what a dump!' Danae gave her verdict. 'The whole place needs razing to the ground.'

'It's not that hopeless,' Kiall told her. 'In the old days it was sort of picturesque.'

'It is now,' Caroline maintained, catching her breath at the wilderness. One couldn't mow a place like that. It needed great machines.

At the base of the stairs was Miss Coddington, waving gaily.

'Good lord, it's Joyce!' exclaimed Danae with a flicker of dismay.

'I met her yesterday,' Caroline said, 'she's my friend.'

'As she was to your mother.' Kiall's voice had lost its humour, hinting at a return to hostilities.

'Morning, everyone!' Joycie called.

'Hi, Joyce.' Kiall gave her a lazy wave.

Danae burst out laughing. 'What on earth has she got on?'

Kiall seemed to chide her. 'Joyce is eccentric, but she's a damn good sort.'

The warmth of his support made Caroline look at him in surprise. He had a beautifully shaped head, ears that were set close to his head. The kind of head, really, to sculpt. It was a thought. Now that miraculously she had been given her freedom she could work at her interests. Pottery, perhaps. There was a thriving creative artists' colony in the North.

This morning Joyce was wearing a Roman senator's toga with outlandish chic. 'Came for you, did he?' She looked down at Caroline with a look of great kindness. 'I didn't think you'd hold out much hope.'

Caroline's green eyes lit up in an answering smile. 'Don't worry, it won't happen again. He tricked me.'

'What's one little kid?' Kiall shrugged his wide shoulders.

Joyce gave Danae a somewhat altered glance. 'How are you, Danae?'

'Very well, Joyce, and you?'

'I could *do* things this morning. . . .' Joyce threw her arms expressively in the air—not a performance, but quite natural. 'Caroline and I will get straight in there and put the house to rights.'

'She's not *staying*, Joycie,' Kiall said.

'But, dear boy. . . .'

'*No*, Joyce.'

'Let's go up and have a dish of tea. I've brought my own.' Joyce swept her toga above her sandalled feet. 'By the way, dear, you left the lights on.'

Caroline came up beside her. 'I was sort of kidnapped,' she explained.

'Really?' Joyce looked thrilled. 'I must tell you what happened to my great-aunt when she was travelling in the Sahara.'

CHAPTER FIVE

'WELL now!' Joyce mopped her brow with a handkerchief stowed away in the toga, 'that's a big improvement!'

They had been working all day and though they were limp with heat and tiredness, the bungalow was starting to look like a real home.

'Please stop, Joyce.' Caroline implored this incredibly efficient lady.

'Shall do, m'dear.' Joyce put a bucket out the back door and slumped on to a kitchen chair. 'As Paddy would say, I'm fair tuckered out.'

'If I were only sure of staying.' Caroline abandoned herself to grim thoughts.

'Buck up, m'dear,' Joyce told her bracingly. 'You do rather well when Kiall's out to rattle you.'

Caroline studied her damp, dust-streaked limbs. 'Not rattle, Joyce. Remove.'

'Then we shall just have to challenge his dictatorial powers.' Joyce regarded her limp toga. 'Well, let's remove the mess, then we'll have dinner at my abode.'

'Gosh!' Caroline exclaimed when she saw it.

'Belonged to one of the sugar barons.' Joyce steamed upwards across the emerald lawns. 'Ah, there you are, Molly, m'girl!' she called heartily.

'But she's beautiful!' Caroline cried, and Molly was—a big golden labrador with a splendid, gentle head and far gone in the figure.

'Lost it, of course, when she was spayed.' Joyce said with the uncanny knack of answering unspoken questions.

'She's beautiful!' Caroline repeated, always a friend to the animals around the convent. 'What a lovely expression!'

Joyce regarded the labrador just as fondly. 'Saved her, you know. Couple up here were going off to South Africa and were going to have her put down. There are more inside. Two cats, Antony and Cleopatra.'

Caroline followed Joyce's curiously regal figure as she walked up the broad flight of steps that led to the admirably constructed timber residence. It was single-storey on stumps, the long main elevation protected by the deep cool verandahs of the tropics.

'But this is delightful, Joyce!' she smiled.

'Goldfields brash. There's plenty of money in the North, you know.'

Inside had been furnished with a great deal of verve and originality. Splendid antiques jostled alongside the most avant-garde seating and a vast collection of paintings and a thousand and one objets d'art.

It was so dramatic, so decorative, Caroline couldn't help staring.

'Always had a flair!' Joyce pronounced. 'At one time Nancy Lancaster, doyen of interior design, you know, asked my advice.'

While Joyce dressed for dinner, Caroline wandered around admiring everything. Great fans swished overhead and here, on the hilltop, it was blessedly cool.

She didn't even see the cat until it leapt at her from behind a two-foot-high Chinese vase.

'Hey, puss, you frightened me!'

'That's Cleo!' Joyce swept back into the resplendent sitting room, wearing a Chinoiserie loose gown she had

had made up in Hong Kong. 'She's only being playful, not attacking.'

Caroline put the big tortoiseshell cat down and it streaked through the wide open door. 'Aren't you frightened she'll knock something over?'

'Mysteriously they never have.' Joyce looked quite unconcerned, even though the Chinese vase was extremely valuable. 'Neat creatures, cats. Very surefooted.'

It turned out to be the most pleasant evening Caroline had ever had. Like her decorating, Joyce's cooking had a dash of genius. Add to that a tremendous sense of humour and the kindest of hearts behind the daunting exterior and Caroline's closely guarded reserve all but collapsed. For some reason, both of them laughed until the tears stood in their eyes.

'For someone so young,' Joyce said sincerely, 'you have a delicious sense of humour.'

Caroline shook her head. 'I've never had one before.'

'Do you remember your father at all?' Joyce asked suddenly.

'Only very vaguely.' *Was* he my father? Caroline was asking herself.

Joyce pursed her lips thoughtfully. 'Ted had that very dry sense of humour. Many was the funny thing he said to me.'

Caroline was quiet for a long time.

'What is it, m'dear?' Joyce was loath to see the radiance go out of that small, wary face.

'There are so many things I don't know, Joyce. Tell me,' Caroline begged.

Beneath the gorgeous folds of her gown, Joyce clenched her hands hard. It was damnable to have to upset the girl.

'I must be very like my mother?' Caroline raised her green eyes.

Surprisingly Joyce shrugged this aside. 'Yes and no. Physically you could be Deborah's double, but your personality is quite different. If it gives you pleasure, although I was very fond of Deborah, I would say you have far more character. More spunk. More backbone.'

'Remember I'm the product of a good boarding school,' Caroline smiled, a little bitterly.

'I'm remembering,' said Joyce, a faraway look to her fine dark eyes.

'Remembering what?'

'How Deborah was when I first met her.'

'Did she really come out from England to marry Martin Stirling?' asked Caroline.

'Well, the Stirlings *are* English, you know. Or rather this branch of the family keeps up very much with their relatives at home. Georgina married an Englishman. Met him, as it happened, at one of the cousin's parties. Lib is with her now—Elizabeth, Kiall's mother. Went to pieces utterly after Newell was killed.'

'There's something you don't want to tell me.' Caroline fixed the older woman with an unwinking gaze.

'All the missing pieces,' Joyce said, and sighed heavily. 'Another cup of coffee, m'dear?'

'I'll pour.' Caroline wasn't going to let her off easily.

Joyce sighed again as if vaguely tormented.

'You *must* tell me, Joyce,' Caroline persisted, 'before somebody else does. Not knowing is the worst part.'

'I suppose you have the right.' Joyce passed a big, shapely hand over her less than sleek chignon. 'You won't like what you hear.'

'You said yourself I've got spunk.' Instinctively

Caroline was bracing herself.

Joyce's strong face lit briefly with hope. 'In any case, it has nothing at all to do with you.'

'The sins of the fathers *are* visited on the children, Joyce,' Caroline said dismally. Wasn't she the living proof?

Joyce put her coffee down on the lotus-shaped Chinese table. 'Perhaps Deborah was a little reckless, foolish—I don't know. I think myself she was so innocent, so certain people were what they seemed to be. She came out to marry Martin, but in the end she ran off with your father. It was a dreadful scandal, but nothing compared to what came after. Instead of staying away, Ted brought her back here to Stirling. It was the greatest mistake. You were scarcely born when the marriage seemed to be foundering.'

Caroline's small chiselled features sharpened with shock. 'Do you mean I was born here?'

'You were.' Joyce's sun tanned face seemed more deeply lined. 'Before you were two, your mother was killed.'

'I don't believe it.' There was pain in Caroline's young voice. 'Why should anyone tell me my mother died when I was born? I always thought it was the reason my father . . . Edward Marshall . . . seemed to hate me.'

'She died in a car crash,' Joyce told her. 'But she wasn't alone. Martin Stirling was with her.'

'What do you mean?' Caroline's green eyes flashed.

'Those are the facts, m'dear. They died together. Went over a cliff at Hunter's Gorge.'

'And why were they together?' Caroline asked.

For just an instant Joyce looked away from her. 'Who knows? Perhaps she asked Martin for help. She should have married him, not your father. It was

Martin she was in love with.'

Caroline bowed her shining head, slipping her hand into the oval neckline of her simple Sunday-best. 'I think you'd better see my locket,' she said.

With her thick eyebrows beetled, Joyce looked ferocious. 'I've seen that before. A charming little piece of Victoriana.'

'It belonged to my mother.'

'I know.' Joyce put out her hand and Caroline dropped the heart-shaped gold locket into her palm.

'I've always believed, since my fourteenth birthday, that the two people inside were my mother and father.'

Joyce, with her acute perceptions, seemed to know what was coming. 'No, m'dear. *No.*' She shook her head emphatically.

'Who would really know?' Caroline herself gave a curiously childlike and frightened gesture.

'Your mother, m'dear, was an exceedingly proper young lady,' said Joyce.

'Who jilted the man she was to marry, then came back to torment him.'

'Ah, no, m'dear,' Joyce said very gently. 'Ted did that. Deborah had to go where her husband decreed. Those were the days when women had to go through the downs with the ups. Now the young brides just up and leave home. The least little thing is said, and it's divorce.'

'You mean Edward Marshall forced her to come back here?' Caroline gazed at her friend with passionate earnestness.

Joyce made a choked sound. 'The worst possible thing he could have done, and I told him so. But Teddy had a cruel streak. He was reared by an aunt, you know. Very little love and affection in the home. A good woman in her way, but with no natural sympathy or feeling for children. Teddy was always a loner. He had nothing. Martin Stirling had the lot. I'd say the moment he set eyes on Deborah he decided to take her away.'

'From a man like Martin Stirling?' If he had been anything like his nephew Caroline would have thought it impossible.

'I suspect Teddy told a few lies. In fact, I *know* he did. When I taxed him with it, he told me it wasn't my concern.'

'But what did he say?' Caroline was unable to keep calm.

'That Martin had other women. What else?'

'And *did* he?'

'I suppose at that time he was the most eligible man in the State. The Stirlings were, and are now, fabulously wealthy. They've had their personal tragedies, but money-wise everything they touch turns to gold. There were a dozen very serious contenders for Martin's hand, gels who were prepared to give Deborah a good run for her money. In the end I think Deborah believed what Ted told her. You couldn't shake Ted with his lies. He was very good at it, and of course, Martin was his own worst enemy, full of a furious pride. He expected Deborah to trust him implicitly. No Stirling ever has had to explain himself. Then there was Barbara Morley, married and long gone away. She and Martin had had something going before he went away to England and met Deborah. Barbara never forgave him, and I believe Teddy carefully cultivated her jealousy for his own ends.'

'Now I *know* he wasn't my father!' Caroline cried. 'I could never have done a thing like that.'

'Love ... desire ... does strange things to people, sends them a little mad. I'm afraid Teddy wanted your mother and there was nothing he wouldn't have done to get her.'

'And he had to come back?'

Joyce nodded gravely. 'The farm was thriving in those days. You wouldn't have known the house—another place altogether. Celia had been a wonderful housekeeper. After Teddy and your mother were married, she went away—I believe after a terrible argument. Everyone was outraged at what Teddy had done. They all blamed him, not Deborah. She gave the impression of being utterly innocent, an angel.'

Caroline stopped to pat Molly, who thumped her tail. 'So when did she begin to see Martin Stirling again?'

'Actually they were very careful to avoid one another.' Joyce seemed to answer deliberately.

'They could have been meeting secretly.'

'They could,' Joyce agreed, 'but I don't think so. Secrecy might have been Teddy's way, but it wasn't Martin's. Don't suppose he played the rejected lover, not Martin. He convinced us all he'd brushed her aside like a worthless little scatterbrain.'

'It's a terrible story, isn't it?' sighed Caroline.

Joyce was forced to agree.

The rest of the week slipped along almost serenely. Workmen came and went—'Mr Stirling sent us'—and Caroline wisely curbed whatever she thought about that. For one thing, four stumps were replaced under the house and that being done the house lost its languid look. The great trees were stripped of excess growth and a wide area around the house cleared by a big mowing machine.

'Couldn't tell ya how many snakes we killed, miss!'

Such news was stupefying. Caroline hadn't seen a one.

Paddy and Joyce drove in and out; Paddy with the news that Mr Stirling had flown to Brisbane—a business trip.

'I was wondering why I hadn't seen him.' Caroline put a long, frosty drink by Paddy's hand.

'He's always flyin' off some place or other. Got a finger in every pie.' Paddy finished his drink in one gulp and looked out across the garden. 'He's a great organiser, isn't he? Really gets on with the job.'

'At least a half a dozen men every day. I wonder why?'

'Wadda ya mean, love?' Paddy held up his glass for a refill.

'Why he's going to so much trouble if he wants to get rid of me?'

'Not surprisin' really,' Paddy told her frankly. 'We get a few death adders around the place.'

'You mean he wants to send me back in one piece? Just that?'

'Who knows?' Paddy shrugged and scratched his bald pate. 'I'll tell ya one thing, this place is lookin' a real home.' He looked with pleasure at the freshly painted planter's chairs, the small table that had been set with a checkered cloth. Joyce, from the magnificence of her own garden and bush house, had supplied Caroline with the most superb plants and hanging baskets, a dazzling world of tropical ferns, gaudy bromeliads and beautiful orchids. There were giant philodendrons too that placed strategically along the verandah made a brilliant show.

'Joyce has been particularly good to me.' Caroline sat down in her own planter's chair. 'In fact, I couldn't have managed without her. Without you both.'

'Should I remind you that me and your dad were good friends?'

Caroline felt a curiously sick lurch. 'What I know of him, Paddy, I can't like.'

'He had problems, ya see,' Paddy explained.

'He had no right to inflict his cruelties on others.'

'But then, love, no one taught him the rules,' Paddy muttered. 'That auntie of his was a real dragon!'

'Joyce said she was a good woman in her way.'

'Just what I said—a dragon. 'Course, she tried to do 'er best by Teddy, but she nagged him so much he tuned out early. It wasn't exactly a cheery 'ousehold, 'er always dustin' every five minutes. A man was frightened to sit down.'

'So why did you like him, my—father?' asked Caroline.

'I suppose because he was a bit of a larrikin. Handsome kid—nearly as handsome as the Stirlings, but without the class. Ya know what I mean? Didn't 'ave the trainin' on all the finer points. Many's the time we went fishin', cut the cards. Didn't drink much, though and when he did it was that bloody wine. Everyone knows beer is far an' away the best drink in the world.'

'Meaning I haven't got any?' Caroline smiled.

'I'll bring ya over a coupla cartons next time I come.'

'I'll save them for you, Paddy.'

By degrees Paddy got himself up. He didn't seem to have any regular employment but enjoyed a leisurely life walking to and fro from the pub. 'By the way, Joycie tells me ya havin' drivin' lessons. Save ya money—I'll teach ya.'

Caroline put her hand briefly on his shoulder. They were of a height. 'You're doing enough for me already, Paddy. Besides, I've already paid the money.' She hadn't, but Paddy behind the wheel was a homicidal maniac.

'Anyway, I'll come over and cut down the bananas for ya. Many's the banana I had up here.'

'Thanks, Paddy.'

Caroline waved him off, muttering when he almost clipped the newly constructed front gate. It was unbelievable, driving as he did, that he hadn't met a sticky end, but then the thought of cars and accidents led her to the terrible fact she could never now forget. Her mother and Martin Stirling had died together in an accident. Her small face, that had been so relaxed and easy when Paddy had been there, fell into lines of despair.

Where was Hunter's Gorge? There had been no opportunity so far to look around the countryside. Her world had been bounded by the giant cane, but she knew that only short drives away there were crater lakes and crystal waterfalls. The North abounded in beauty spots; magnificent countryside and spectacular views. Perhaps Hunter's Gorge was somewhere near the falls, or one of the mysterious crater lakes. As soon as she could drive a car she would explore. Joyce was planning trips, she knew, but when she saw Hunter's Gorge for the first time, she wanted to be alone.

It was in the town, on one of her very enjoyable shopping expeditions, that she encountered Danae Edgeley again. The department store was quiet, so Danae's clarion tones directed every head.

'Well, if it isn't Miss Marshall!'

The words echoed on and on like a terrible charge.

'How are you?' Caroline nodded curtly. She had a reasonably good idea Danae was her enemy, so she didn't smile.

'Whatever have you got there?' Danae's bright blue eyes roamed Caroline's purchases like a store detective.

'Just a few things for the house.' Caroline answered quietly, not missing the way people were now staring at her. Marshall. *Marshall*. An old lady was looking at her with an inquisitorial eye.

'Unfortunate that you won't be staying.' Danae laughed indulgently. 'Still, we'll do our best to entertain you while you're here.'

'I'll be much too busy for that,' Caroline said rather pointedly. 'As it is I have curtains, slip covers to make.'

'Dear girl,' Danae drawled languidly, 'don't precipitate a Situation. Stay a couple of months if you like, but in the end, Kiall will have his way.'

'About what?' Caroline asked explosively, momentarily forgetting where she was.

Danae took her by the arm and started to move her on. 'Really, dear, you're hopeless, aren't you? You can't continue to stay out at the farmhouse by yourself. It's really not suitable. I ought to tell you we get a lot of hippies and drifters passing through.'

'Well, I've got a gun,' shrugged Caroline.

'You've *what*?' Danae was most certainly shocked.

'Don't worry, I'm not trigger-happy.'

'But this is fearful!' Danae bit on her full under lip.

'Joyce gave it to me,' Caroline explained kindly, 'but first she showed me exactly how to use it. Extraordinary woman, Joyce.'

'You mean she's downright odd!'

'If she is, I like oddities!' Caroline actually smiled. 'If you'll excuse me, Miss Edgeley, I have a bus to catch.' She didn't, but she was expert at quick exits.

'Then please let me drive you home,' Danae said warmly. 'I'm dying to see all you've done.'

In the face of Danae's dogged determination, what was Caroline to do? Danae escorted her to her car, a

pretty little Porsche, took her parcels completely out
of her hands and stowed them away in the rear end of
the sporty little hatchback.

'Some car!' commented Caroline.

'I always travel in the lap of luxury,' Danae told her
superbly.

'I'd never have the pocket money.'

'I do work, you know.' Danae told her rather
sharply. 'It's not easy running the house and playing
hostess for my father. He's an important business man
and Kiall's partner in a half a dozen ventures.'

'And your mother?' Danae asked questions. Why
shouldn't she?

'My mother and father divorced a few years ago.
Daddy and I have the luck to be alone now.'

'Luck?' Caroline enquired wryly, 'to be without your
mother?'

'We never saw eye to eye and she was no help whatever to Daddy.'

'In that case, why not give her the chop!' Caroline
turned her head and looked the older girl full in the
eye. It was devastating to think anyone could possibly
wish to get rid of their mother!

'Mmm,' Danae hummed. 'It was a bit distressing at
the time, but now we're managing beautifully.'

The little Porsche covered the ground to the farmhouse in record time, the owner purring with satisfaction. 'Daddy gave it to me for my last birthday.'

'You must be a daddy's girl?' Caroline reflected.

'Well, obviously, darling, you were not!' Danae's
blue eyes glinted with maliciousness.

So she dislikes me as much as I dislike her, Caroline
thought with no great perception. But why? To begin
with there was a big difference between them; possibly
eight years and a great deal in good fortune. Danae

looked what she was—the adored daughter of a wealthy business man. In fact she had it all together—looks, money, position and a great deal of chic. Today she was dressed in a very simple wraparound dress, but the material was silk crêpe de chine and there was a beautiful bronze leather tie belt around her slender waist. Her minimal make-up was exquisitely perfect with the gleaming, healthy skin betraying no shine.

How does she *do* it? Caroline thought, almost wilting like a cut lily on a stalk. And just look at my dress! She almost wished now she had done some shopping for herself instead of the house. She looked what *she* was; a convent-reared waif.

When Danae saw the farmhouse she looked surprised. In fact, any feigned attempt at friendliness vanished from sight. 'Of course I know Kiall is a very responsible man, but this is carrying things too far,' she said tartly.

'I beg your pardon?' To Caroline's immense satisfaction that came out most impressively. What she lacked in inches she made up in voice production.

Even Danae was taken aback, though she didn't try for a bit of tact. She got out of the car and stared around her incredulously. One could hardly credit so much had been done in such a short space of time.

'I think it was the death adders,' Caroline offered helpfully.

'What on earth are you talking about?' Danae rounded on her sharply.

'Why,' Caroline opened wide her green eyes, 'Mr Stirling being so responsible he couldn't actually let me be bitten!'

'I suppose that's a point.' Danae, too, seemed anxious to clutch at an excuse. It would appear Kiall Stirling was exclusively hers, including his good deeds.

'Shall we go up?' Caroline kept a smile off her fastidious little face.

'But how charming!' Danae purred kindly. 'All those dear little pot plants!'

'Joyce gave them to me.'

'They make everything so cosy!'

Inevitably Caroline was forced into offering a cold drink or perhaps tea, and Danae, wanting the extra time, told the younger girl tea would be best.

'No sugar. A slice of lemon.'

After she had put her parcels down, Caroline dashed through to her bedroom to run a comb through her hair. Danae with her slick perfection made her feel like a real urchin. Behind her closed door she studied her face covertly. Extraordinarily she didn't notice any drooping, but then Danae had pepped up her adrenaline. She looked young, in a far too humble dress, but there was nothing wrong with her face.

'I can't help feeling you've done the wrong thing coming up here,' Danae said almost despairingly as she sipped at her lemon tea. 'Nobody really wants to drag up the old tragedies.'

'Ah well, I've got to live somewhere.' Caroline tried to keep her tender mouth from stiffening.

'Of course it's Thea you'll make suffer.' Danae gazed at her starkly. 'Kiall was just a boy, but obviously Thea remembers everything in the most terrible detail.'

'The mere fact that my mother and Martin Stirling happened to be in the same car proves nothing.' Caroline said hardily.

'*Please*, dear,' Danae interrupted. 'It was confirmed that Martin and your mother picked up their affair.'

'Nobody really knows.' Caroline was overpowered by the desire to protect her dead mother. 'Joyce told me they scarcely spoke a dozen words after my mother and . . . father were married.' Just the slightest hesitation before father, and she would have to stop that.

'Oh, for God's sake don't be so naïve! Joyce *would* say that. She befriended your mother, and I can tell you she had a soft spot for your father.'

'But you were only a child yourself.' Caroline pushed back in her planter's chair.

'Thea and I have had a heart-to-heart talk. *She* knew what happened. Martin Stirling was her brother, her beloved brother. It's too, *too* awful for her to have you here.'

'So what do you want me to do?' Caroline could see that it might be awful.

'Relax for a few weeks and then go on home. We're ready for the cyclone season, you know. My dear, you simply won't be safe!'

For an hour after Danae left, Caroline was still biting her lip. How could anything work out for a girl like herself? Everything about her background had been wretched from the start. Of course it was embarrassing for the Stirlings to have her here. Even the question of her parentage was almost unbearable. Could she possibly be Martin Stirling's child? There was absolutely no way to find out and be discreet. The greatest thing in life for her would have been to have a family. Could the Stirlings possibly be *family*? Orphan or no, she almost shuddered. Thea Stirling would make a singularly mordant aunt and she didn't really want to be Kiall Stirling's cousin; her jumbled-up feelings weren't in the least cousinly. She kept thinking of him at the oddest times. Like now. She began hurriedly to distract herself, cutting out curtains.

Towards dusk he startled her, appearing out of nowhere like the devil. She was working in what she hoped would be a prolific vegetable garden and of course she was grimy with exotic streaks of volcanic soil along her nose and her right cheekbone where she had swiped at a mosquito.

'Hi!' said Kiall, giving her a sharply amused glance.

'Hi!' she returned shortly, immediately on the defensive and wondering why.

'You don't have to grub around like a little market gardener.' He sauntered over a little farther and lifted her to her feet.

'Actually I'm very domesticated.' She looked up at him a little cautiously. Why did he have to be so tall? Or for that matter so stunningly male? He was making her legs feel all rubbery.

'So you're still keen on staying here?' he asked.

'I *am*.'

'Let me see your hand.' His silver eyes narrowed. A man accustomed to having his own way.

'It's nothing.' She wasn't going to show him a silly blister.

'*Show* me.'

Caroline put out her hand, realising it was impossible to resist.

'That looks nasty.' He seemed extremely irritated all of a sudden. 'Worse, the skin is broken.'

'I'll never do the washing up again,' she said flippantly.

'Come inside,' he ordered, quelling her with a look.

So she had to suffer his ministrations like a little girl. 'Thank you.'

He still held her hand. 'When are you eighteen?' he asked.

'Me?' She was really terrified of meeting his eyes. Of course, locked away as she had been from the male of the species it was only natural she would be dreadfully susceptible on exposure.

'Yes, *you*!' he said dryly.

'March.' She very nearly moaned, rattled to the extent she wanted to jerk her injured hand away. 'Don't you know?'

'Don't be stupid,' he said. 'You're not my little cousin.'

'You mean you don't *want* me to be.' She threw up her head and caught the flash of a brilliant anger in his eyes.

'Have you so little regard for your mother? Married to one man and bearing another man's child?'

'Who am I to judge?' Caroline cried out compulsively. 'She was human, wasn't she? Does making a single terrible mistake make her wicked?'

Kiall flinched almost as though she had struck him. 'Hell, do you want to be my cousin?'

He was gripping her so hard she closed her eyes with the pain. 'I want to know about my parents!' she cried defiantly. 'I want a family.'

'Don't think you're fooling me, and don't think you're going to drag my family name through the mud. You're Caroline *Marshall*.'

'Would you let me go?' she asked emotionally.

'I'm sorry.' His silver eyes studied the red marks on her arms. She would have a dozen bruises—more, if she didn't send him away.

'Who really put you up to this?' Kiall asked with deceptive quietness.

'I'm getting sick of this!' She felt enveloped by his physical presence, a prisoner. 'No one put me up to anything. Edward Marshall left me this house. I have nowhere else to go. When I first came here I thought he *was* my father.'

'You need a psychiatrist,' he said brutally.

'Maybe I do,' she said wryly. 'I had a fairly deprived

childhood. You've *got* to understand.'

'I understand I'm not going to let history repeat itself.'

Something in his face made her feel shocked. Trembling, she sank into a chair. 'Please let me stay,' she said faintly.

'So you can hurt more people? I'll wind up killing you,' he gritted.

'For something I'm not responsible for?' She looked into his silver, slitted eyes.

'Enough now,' he said angrily. 'Wash your face.'

'Why?' She was gripping the table so hard, her small hand looked bleached.

'For one thing, it's dirty. For another, I'm taking you for a little run in my car.'

Still trembling, she stood up. 'From the look on your face, I won't be coming back.'

'I just thought it might do more good than all the talk.'

In the bathroom, with her hair down, Caroline scrubbed her face clean.

'Here.' Kiall had followed her, passing her the towel.

Every minute brought more disturbing sensations. She didn't even come up to his shoulder. More, she had to tip her head right back to look up at him.

'At least let me put on a dress,' she said faintly.

'Another of those ones you ran up at the convent?'

'What else?' She was glad he had moved back so she could pass him.

'I'll bet you didn't wear those shorts there.'

It was unnatural the way she was reacting, proving the case against overwhelming sheltering. Yet when Ian Randall had taken her to dinner she had almost

recoiled from his interest. 'Go away!' she snapped, very
nearly violently.

She put on her pink dress that completely lacked
style. Style and wealth—they weren't for the likes of
her. She took her long hair and twisted it into a coil. It
was beautiful hair, she supposed, but better short in
the heat.

When she went back into the sitting room Kiall was
still standing. Again that hard, measuring look.

'Isn't the heat appalling?' She couldn't think of anything else.

'I don't notice it.' He looked every inch above such
minor discomforts.

'I think I'll get my hair cut.' She twisted up a nervous hand.

'Don't try it.'

His tone made her look at him in surprise. 'But it
would be cooler.'

'What's wrong with the way you've got it now?'

His concentration on her face and her hair made her
feel unnerved. 'Surely I don't have to check with you
if I want to get my hair cut?'

'You'll do well the way you are.' He gave a harsh,
sardonic laugh. 'Now, let's go!'

CHAPTER SIX

'WHERE *are* we going?' she asked him as they swept past the canefields.

'Where neither of us can pretend.' Kiall's sheened glance looked dangerous.

'I think I'm frightened of you,' Caroline confessed.

'Then you're showing a bit of sense.'

It was hard to sound spirited when inside she was panic-stricken. 'You're surely not thinking of dropping me in the lake? I'm an excellent swimmer.'

There was a bitter twist to his faint smile. 'When you go back to where you came from, take up acting,' he said dryly. 'I've a feeling you'll be awfully good at it. Among other things.'

'Such as?'

He caught her eyes briefly. 'It's not the right time to talk about it.'

'Then write to me.' She brushed back a strand of her blonde hair and looked at his profile. The hard, handsome face had a brooding look to it, and she felt a flash of total unreality. She had lived with that face day and night since her fourteenth birthday. Accepting that he didn't belong to her in some way was a hard thing to do. He didn't seem unfamiliar to her, but someone she had always been locked to, someone who held her in thrall.

So intense were her thoughts, it took her some minutes to realise the cane had given way to tropical jungle. They were climbing. Parrots were following them, flashing in and out of the trees in bejewelled splendour, and beyond, the massive rain forest mountains where waterfalls cascaded into emerald green lakes.

'It's beautiful, isn't it?' she breathed with a sudden breath of awe. A white mist was swirling over the highest peaks like a streaming veil and the burning sky was so radiant she had to half close her eyes.

'Unique,' said Kiall, almost gently, when he was not a gentle man. 'The tropical rain forest of the kind that exists in our part of the world is the most luxuriant, diverse and complex community of plants on the face of the earth. It takes a lifetime to appreciate it.'

'You love it, don't you?'

'You sound shocked.' His brilliant glance determined her expression. 'Don't you think I could love anything?'

'Maybe your children, when they're born,' Caroline admitted.

'You've a lot of wisdom for very little experience.'

'I've a lot of knowledge of a life without love,' she shrugged.

'For that your father should have been whipped off his feet!'

When she saw the anger on his face, she sighed. Coming up here had somehow eased her own burden, made her more compassionate. 'If Edward Marshall loved my mother as much as I've been told he did, life must have been very barren without her.'

'He could have rejoiced in his daughter.'

'Maybe he feared I wasn't his at all. Maybe he knew.'

'You're just a little girl crying in the dark,' he said sombrely. 'Foolish as your mother was, I'm sure no thought of infidelity entered her head. And you never knew Martin. He had the pride of a black angel. He even looked like one, and he could have had any woman he wanted. Why would he bother with a little fool who betrayed him?'

'Maybe she was part of him.' The words leapt from her mouth.

'Say another word and I'll strangle you!'

Now the trees soared above them to the sky, great colonnades that reduced the brilliant light to a golden-green gloom.

'You do want to frighten me, don't you?' Caroline asked quietly, matching her voice to the all pervading hush.

'Perhaps a little.' He didn't look at her as she laid her head back against the seat. Her eyes were as large and wary as a gazelle's.

'I think I know now where you're taking me,' she said.

'Hold the picture in your mind.'

'Why are you being so cruel?' she cried. 'You've nothing to fear from me. I'm seventeen years old and I'm quite alone.'

'And a peril to us all,' Kiall returned curtly. 'Do you think it's wise for a young girl to live alone? How long do you think it's going to be before the men come calling?'

'I've got a gun,' she said flatly.

'Don't try levelling it at *me*.' His sparkling eyes touched her. 'Joyce is a swift mover. I suppose she gave it to you.'

'She did. And she showed me how to use it, clean and load it. She's a very good teacher and I'm an apt pupil.'

'We'll see about that when we get back,' he snapped.

Now the forest-filled gorges were dropping away

from beneath them, the luxuriant green slashed with purple shadows. Wonderful scenery that, remembering, made her mouth go dry. Why would they ever have come up here in the first place? It was far from the town.

In a cleared area where the clean trunks of the rose gums soared, Kiall stopped the car. Behind that was a wall of vines and a million bird calls. Epiphytic orchids were flourishing, growing in the forks of trees and on rocks close to the ground, and as Caroline slid out of the car and looked upwards she saw a beautiful cream and gold orchid cascading its strongly scented six-feet-long sprays from a distance of thirty or more feet.

Here in the uplands it was much cooler and, except for the powerful voices of the birds, so still.

'Why have you got to spoil it?' she begged him.

'So the innocent won't continue to be punished.'

'And I'm *not* innocent?' She threw her head back in a proud way.

'You're beautiful,' he said sharply. 'With cat's eyes.'

'Sad eyes, can't you see? Not wicked.'

His dark face looked implacable. 'I want to spare you too, Caroline.'

It was the first time he had ever called her by her name and she felt as if she had no skin, no protective coating at all.

'I hate you,' she said softly.

'I know you do.' He gave a brittle laugh. 'Either one of us could ruin the other's life.'

The admission, brought out into the open, slashed through her like a searing knife. 'So show me,' she said a little wildly. 'So show me this place.'

'Long ago,' he said strangely. 'It was so long ago, yet it's so close.'

'They should both be here!' Caroline shouted. 'Why

did they have to die?'

Her clear young voice startled the birds. They rose in great flocks, glorious, wheeling, flashing colours then returned to the trees.

Grim-faced, Kiall walked away from her, over the masses of fallen leaves, and Caroline followed in his track. Little plumes of mist skeined the interlacing canopy and just a single tree was covered with an amazing species of plants; ferns, orchids, mosses, lichens. There were many ridges, many gorges, and now underfoot the luminous jungle fungi.

'Wait for me!' she called. Masses of ferns were gathering around her, great banks of lilies, ropes of liane and lawyer vines that dipped in threatening festoons. All this beauty she only saw with half an eye, she was so disturbed.

There was a waterfall somewhere. Now she heard its dull roar.

When Kiall took her hand it was a shock. Their skin joined together. Their story. They really were linked together by the same tragedy. The thought left her stricken and she knew he could feel the trembling that was running right through her body.

Suddenly through the screen of giant tree ferns she saw the white torrent that spilled on to moss-covered boulders and spread into a deep pool. The cliffs to either side were covered with great lilies with sabre-like leaves. There were four more waterfalls, but she knew this was the one. It fell forty feet down the almost perpendicular slope, a silver slash in the lofty green jungle, a place of unearthly beauty; fern and orchid and vine.

In her mind, she had a picture of them coming here. Had Kiall taken her hand? Her own hand was shaking badly and though he held it tightly there was no comfort from his savage hurt. Of course he had idolised his uncle; the tone of his voice had told her that. Time would never remove the pain. Or the blame. She could say without hesitation that it was the worst moment of her life.

Slowly and resolutely she went with him, just a little farther, away from the lake and along the scenic road. A few yards from the edge of the cliff she screamed like a child pursued by demons, and when he caught her she crashed her small fists into his chest.

'It had to be an accident. No one could die *that* way!'

'Everyone knew the road was dangerous.'

'But it isn't!' They had negotiated it without much difficulty.

'It was years ago!' Kiall was shouting as she was, shaking her while she quivered like a leaf.

She was quite mad with grief. It was a nightmare now. The wild beauty—the old horror.

'They loved each other.' Instead of condemning, she felt a terrible ache of sadness.

'Love, lust, what the hell!' He was bitterly angry.

'What do *you* know?' she cried wildly. 'I don't think for a moment you've ever loved any woman.'

'But I know how to make love,' he said furiously. 'Make love, play love, talk love. Even kiss a stupid child.'

Caroline began to laugh, a laugh that hurt her, and brutally he stopped her mouth. He held her head tight, twisting her long hair around his fingers, while she held her face up, wishing she could die.

'I want to hurt you. Pay you back.'

She felt his lips force hers apart, and out of the bitter anger that flared between them came arousal. She couldn't not give him what he wanted—a deeper and deeper exploration of her mouth. His hands had moved from her hair, down her back, moulding her to him, half lifting her off the ground. It was punishment, shattering, but she wanted it as much as he did.

'Say you'll go away.'

Her pulsing mouth couldn't make the words come.

He kissed her again, a sensual assault full of passion, but nothing of tenderness or hope, and all the time she did nothing, but let him drain himself of his anger.

When she finally opened her eyes, he was looking at her, his eyes so brilliant they were like diamonds.

'I don't know who I hate the most,' he muttered.

'I don't hate you,' she said.

'You're crying.'

'I never cry.' She blinked and the tears fell on to her cheeks.

'Enemies, that's what we are, Caroline, you and I.' He bent his head and to her shock took her tears upon his tongue.

She sagged against him then, wondering if she was going to faint.

'I'm a swine, aren't I?' he said.

She was incapable of answering, allowing herself to be swept up into his arms.

'Just think if you were someone else but yourself.'

She turned her head into his chest and he gave a terrible, strangled laugh.

She had to talk to someone. Joyce.

It was the next morning and Caroline went straight into town. From there she took another bus, then trudged up the hill to the big white house that jutted out like a proud bird.

'But, m'dear little gel!' Joyce exclaimed on her arrival, 'whatever is the matter?'

'I need advice, Joyce.' It calmed her just to look into Joyce's distinguished, kindly face.

She didn't know it, but she looked as pale and silvery as a wraith.

'Come in, come in.' Joyce drew her into the splendidly cluttered drawing room. 'Just sit down and don't say a word while I make you a cup of tea. M'dear, you look exhausted, and there are shadows under those beautiful eyes.'

Why not? Caroline let her lids fall. I never slept a wink. Every minute, every second, she had relived that experience in the forest. The singing blood . . . the fainting away. Now she could understand the storms of passion, the terrible consequences they could bring. It was possible to forget everyone—everything. Honour, virtue, loyalty, everything tossed aside. The constancy of a lifetime to count for nothing. Passion could be annihilating; she knew that now.

'I've decided to go away, Joyce,' she said quietly, when Joyce came back to sit down beside her.

'Tell me what's happened.' Joyce squeezed her hand.

'I'm not wanted here, that's all.'

'Nonsense!' said Joyce stoutly. 'I'm going to give a party for you. You'll see. Invite all the young folk. It will be marvellous. I love young people around me, they're so vital.'

'Kiall wants me to go,' Caroline said in that same, too quiet voice. 'And he is, without question, the boss.'

'You mean he's told you in so many words?' Joyce stared at nothing in particular.

'You can see, looking as I do, he might hate me.'

'Rubbish!' Joyce contradicted. 'You've a glorious little face! Wish I'd had it as a gel.'

'It's the wrong face,' Caroline said quietly, and suddenly put her head down into her arms and cried.

'There, there,' Joyce held her so bracingly, it hurt. 'I can quite see the difficulties, you're so like Deborah, but after a little while people will forget. The youngsters aren't that interested anyway.'

'I don't want to stay, Joycie.' Caroline's voice was muffled by her arms.

'What's he done to you?' Joyce asked in an aggressively protective voice. 'There's a devil in Kiall, occasionally. I've seen it before.'

Caroline sat up and absently rubbed her cheeks. 'We can't pretend it doesn't matter, Joyce. The sight of me distressed his aunt dreadfully and even he's not immune.'

'I'm afraid that's not reason enough to send you away. Where will you go? You're a young girl on your own.'

'I had the impression, Timbuctoo.'

'That's the spirit!' said Joyce, applauding the attempt at humour. 'You know, it might be an idea to move out of the farmhouse. I know for a fact Kiall has declared it out of bounds.'

'For whom?'

'Oh, you know, the lads.' Joyce regarded her with faint surprise. 'Do you never look in your mirror, m'dear?'

'All the vanity has been trained out of me.' Caroline felt inexplicably aggrieved. 'Do you mean to tell me . . .?'

'I do,' Joyce nodded sagely. 'Kiall has tremendous dictatorial powers. If he hadn't spoken, many the lad would have trundled out to the farm. Green-eyed blondes are as scarce as hen's teeth.'

'It all seems so terribly autocratic.'

'It *is*,' Joyce agreed. 'Maybe some day he'll mellow. Anyway, m'dear, it's all for your own good. I've been worried about you there m'self. And poor old Paddy has never stopped in his own words, bashing my ear. Little gels like you can't hide yourselves without a trace.'

'But it's my home, Joyce. My only home.'

'Why not come to me?' Joyce said gently. 'It's lonely, sometimes, clattering around a big house. I'd be very glad of your company and it might mollify Kiall a fraction. He's genuinely worried about your living at the farmhouse by yourself. Enough to issue a pretty dire warning.'

'Wouldn't that make everyone more terribly curious?'

'Yes, m'dear. But from a distance. Young men have been known to get out of hand and one look would tell them you're as innocent as a newborn babe.' Joyce jumped up, apparently struck by her brilliant idea. 'I know you're loving the feeling of having your own little place, but the fact is, you might make Kiall happier if you came to me.'

'He wants me out!' Caroline shuddered, just remembering.

'You haven't fallen in love with him, have you?' Joyce turned and transfixed her with her fine eyes.

'Not precisely,' said Caroline. 'I hate him.'

'I keep thinking now it can't happen again.' Joyce sat down again and picked up the teapot with a shaky hand. 'Don't ever fall in love with Kiall,' she warned.

'How could I?' Caroline asked. 'I wouldn't set my sights so low.'

Joyce set the pot down with a clash and burst out laughing. 'Oh, I *do* like your sense of humour! Just like Teddy's.'

'I wish somebody could really prove to me that Edward Marshall was my father,' sighed Caroline.

'You want proof?' Joyce affected a stern, judicial look. 'You've come to the right place. I knew your father well.'

'You knew Martin Stirling too.'

'Be a good girl,' Joyce sighed, 'and have a little faith. Deborah may háve bitterly regretted her marriage. She may have told Martin, finally, of her troubles, she may have even told him again that she loved him, but she didn't betray Teddy. Never in the early days of their marriage. Unthinkable. I tell you, I *knew* her. I knew them all. No matter what Martin thought, he never went near her. It was sheer desperation that drove Deborah to him. Teddy, though he had her, drove them both mad with his jealousies. He was forever talking about how he took Deborah off Martin. Handsome, clever, dashing Martin. No one had ever managed to best Martin. He was very articulate, Teddy—as you are. He had that little bitter twist to his tongue, a by-product of being unhappy.'

'He took me there.' Caroline said despairingly.

'Where, m'dear?' Joyce was genuinely mystified.

'Hunter's Gorge.'

'For God's sake,' Joyce said testily. 'For God's sake! Kiall's not a cruel man.'

'He is to me,' Caroline said dully. 'I'm his enemy.'

'Nevertheless he's done a great deal to help you,' Joyce nodded her head several times, gravely. 'Of course the tragedy sent us all a little mad. No one could believe it, let alone accept it. Martin was so incredibly vital, alive. No one could believe they weren't coming back.'

'Was it an accident, Joyce?' Caroline's green eyes were strangely expressionless in her pale face.

'Of course it was.' Joyce stared up at a painting.

'Kiall told me the road was very dangerous at that time.'

'I told you, m'dear,' Joyce gave her a deeply compassionate look, 'it was an accident. Martin Stirling was the last man on earth to contemplate a suicide pact. Not Martin, a man of action. Besides, Deborah had you. There was never a more loving little mother. You'd better remember that.'

'Then how did it happen?' Caroline was unwilling to rely on faith alone.

'Human error.' Joyce spoke with the voice of authority. 'There were skid marks all over the green slime. For some reason Deborah was at the wheel. It *was* her car, or rather Teddy's, but Martin wasn't the sort of man who was happy as a woman's passenger. Obviously Deborah resisted his taking the wheel, and that was her last mistake. The car went over the gorge.'

Both of them had their heads leaning back against the sofa and Caroline closed her eyes. 'Maybe she wanted to take him with her.'

'No,' Joyce said shakily. 'Deborah could never have hurt anyone. At worst, she was strung up, overwrought. It was an accident—that was the finding.'

'To save talk,' Caroline murmured miserably.

'Leave it alone, Caroline,' Joyce urged. 'Don't ask questions for which there are no answers. What happened is over, in the past. You have your whole future in front of you. Don't let the old tragedies destroy you. Come to me for a little while. What about it? I'll tell Kiall.'

'He won't agree.'

Strangely he did, and by the end of the week Caroline had moved in with Joyce. Now, it seemed, 'the lads', as Joyce kept calling them, were free to drop in on the white house. There were so many visitors, after a while, Joyce declared she wasn't going to open the door.

'We'll have a party, get it all over at once.'

Caroline felt more than a little frightened. Here she was, like a wild thing lying low, and Joyce was talking about presenting her to the town.

'Of course you'll need some decent clothes.'

'I don't want a party, Joyce!' Caroline protested.

'Of course you do!' Joyce waved a hand in dismissal. 'Every young gel has a coming out party. Nothing will make me happier than to present you. I have the most wonderful material I'll have May Wong make up. Genius, May, makes the most exquisite garments.'

Was it worth it to risk Kiall Stirling's displeasure? Sleep never came to Caroline that she didn't dream of him—not pleasant dreams, but dreams that she had to fling off like nightmares. She was terribly afraid of him. Afraid of herself.

One afternoon Thea Stirling called on them in an agitated state.

'How could you, Joyce?' They were seated inside the drawing room, the atmosphere thundery inside and out.

'How could I what, Thea?' Joyce asked blandly.

'Have you no memory?'

A restlessness was upon Joyce. She swept up from the couch, impressive in a richly coloured cotton garment. 'Sometimes we have to let go of our memories.'

'Never!' Miss Stirling protested. 'I've always liked you, Joyce, but you're an arrogant woman. You tamper with people's lives.'

'And you don't, Thea?' Joyce challenged magnificently. 'You did your best to come between

Deborah and Martin.'

'She wasn't good enough for him.' Miss Stirling looked ill.

'He trusted you, Thea,' Joyce said grimly.

'Must this . . . girl be here?' Thea Stirling threw out a hand without ever once looking in Caroline's direction.

'Yes,' Joyce said firmly, and compressed her straight mouth. 'Why don't you practise some sisterly love?'

'That's impossible, Joyce, and you know it.' Thea Stirling let her hand drop. 'I can never forget how I lost my beloved brother.'

'After all, Caroline is in no way responsible.'

'Maybe not,' the other woman sighed. 'Yet in all the years since Martin died, I've been waiting for this girl to turn up.'

'Why?' Caroline was startled into crying.

A deep flush mounted to Thea Stirling's high cheek bones, but still she didn't look Caroline's way. 'To learn the truth.'

'I've told her,' Joyce said abruptly.

'Then tell *me*.' Thea laughed a little strangely.

'You're neurotic, Thea.' Joyce looked down at the rigidly convulsed woman. 'You won't let the past lie. You keep it alive.'

'Why did she have to come here?'

'You answered that yourself.' Caroline spoke again. Her beautiful skin had acquired a golden tint against which her green eyes and pale hair were startling.

'In the meantime,' Thea Stirling cried, still in that distraught voice, 'you throw parties.'

'Caroline has every right to a normal life. It's been pretty miserable so far.'

'Let things alone, Joyce,' said Caroline quietly.

Joyce was looking more and more irritable. 'You like

things to be miserable.'

Thea Stirling didn't speak, didn't move.

'I don't like hurting people, Miss Stirling,' said Caroline, and the distress stood in her green eyes, 'but I have a right to live where I like.'

'Of course you do!' Joyce exclaimed heartily.

'I know you're out to make trouble,' Miss Stirling muttered. 'Danae thinks so too.'

'And you know why!' Joyce snorted. 'She's terrified of anyone who might flutter their eyelashes at Kiall. My God, how many friendships have you ruined for him? From the time he was a boy. You and your poison, Thea. Lib rarely saw it. You worked hard to be friends with your sister-in-law.'

'I'm friends with everyone.' Thea Stirling rose also, with drama. 'I see I can't appeal to you, Joyce. For all your intelligence you're not a woman of good sense.'

'Perhaps you're right. I let you in.'

Thea Stirling smiled tightly. 'I shall tell Kiall what you said.'

'Thea, m'dear,' Joyce replied violently, 'Kiall knows all about you.'

On the day of the party, Paddy and a few of his mates came over to do the lawn. Or rather, Paddy did the directing and his amiable friends did the mowing. And there was plenty to do. The house stood on almost an acre of ground and the grass grew so prolifically it would have become jungle in under a month.

'Strewth, it's hot!' Paddy muttered from the cover of the iron lace gazebo.

'Aren't you going to give your friends a hand?' Caroline enquired slyly.

'I've got ten years on them,' Paddy told her confidentially. 'Besides, I'll go barmy with the sun on me bald head.'

Caroline broke a bright blue trumpet from the showy morning glories and thrust it through her hair. 'I'm nervous about tonight, Paddy.'

'Jest keep lookin' in the mirror.' Paddy beat at a cloud of iridescent insects.

'I've got the most beautiful dress,' she went on in a worried voice. 'Joyce has enough bolts of material to open a shop.'

'A collector, our Joycie.' Paddy gave her a good-humoured grin. 'Got 'em in Hong Kong, I expect. She's always dashin' over. Money's no problem with Joycie. A woman of means.'

'She's being terribly kind to me.'

'And you're good for 'er,' Paddy insisted. 'Joycie loves people, parties. And she sure knows 'ow to give 'em—the best tucker, the best drink. Yair, I'd say Joycie was a lady of real style. Eccentric, mind you, but a real lady. She was a tower of strength in the last blow. Ya can depend on Joycie to keep her head.'

The mowing and clipping over, the boys sat out in the gazebo and drank cold beer.

'Looks a picture, don't it?' Paddy said complacently, and they all breathed a deep sigh of contended agreement. Everything about Joycie Coddington's was magnificent. In a region that abounded in 'characters' Joyce had made her mark.

CHAPTER SEVEN

By nine-thirty it was certain that Kiall did not intend to arrive. Perversely, though Caroline had dreaded their next encounter she was hollow with disappointment. Even Joyce kept looking continually towards the front door.

He's not coming, Caroline thought. He won't see me in this dress. Her shining hair fell down her back, this after long consideration with Joyce, and the dress she was wearing had won everyone's startled approval. She looked stunningly beautiful, but still very young.

Amid the general din of music and laughter and voices she moved with an ease that surprised her. A few people had looked at her very oddly, but these were the older guests, the people who remembered her mother. One rather pretty but faded little woman stared at her for most of the time—nothing condemning, but insistent, and afterwards Joyce told her that, before Deborah, Fiona Fraser had been 'the big interest in Teddy's life.'

The complications of love.

The dozen and more eligible young men Joyce had invited gathered around her, but she did not invite any one of them closer—to the great relief of the girls. None of them could believe they now had so much competition, but it was clear Miss Coddington's protégée was anything but a flirt. If anything, she was charming, but rather reserved.

A sigh of relief. No one really wanted to be bitchy, but sometimes a girl had to be. The newcomer, though beautiful, seemed strangely non-combatant. Either that, or she was immune to their handsome beaux.

It was an older man who made a determined effort to single Caroline out—and being older, succeeded.

'Incredible how like your mother you are,' he told her.

'You knew her?' He couldn't have been more than thirty-two or three. Kiall's age, she told herself.

'Of course,' he said ironically. 'She was the sort of woman you don't forget.'

'But you must have been a boy?'

He took her arm, leading her to a chair on the terrace. 'Fifteen—almost a man. She had that same moonlit hair, the green eyes.'

'I really don't want to talk about her now,' Caroline said.

'I understand.' He looked at her indulgently. 'What a beautiful dress. It suits you perfectly.'

'A present from Joyce.' Caroline was suddenly overcome by melancholy. What hope was there for her to want what she was never meant to have? Absently she smoothed a fold of her beautiful circular skirt, gold and green and violet; a bolt from a cedarwood chest, sewn into beauty.

'You seem unhappy?'

'No.' She looked up quickly and smiled, her pale golden hair in the half light alloyed with silver. 'Thoughtful, perhaps. Wondering at Joyce's kindness and understanding.'

'Surely you'd be very easy to be kind to.' He was staring at her keenly, but not, Caroline thought, in an entirely friendly way. For a moment she was tempted to ask him why *he* didn't really like her.

There was no time for further reflections because through the wide open french doors she saw a familiar figure. A deeply familiar figure.

'Why, what's the matter?' Colin Rayment turned to follow the direction of her widened gaze. 'Oh, Kiall,' he said flatly. 'Everyone stops dead for him.'

'You don't enjoy his company?' she asked.

'Yes, I do. I just envy him so much.'

It made sense. Kiall Stirling was a very impressive man.

'Of course he's got Danae in tow,' he added.

'And it bothers you?' she asked demurely.

'I might as well admit it.' A wry smile lit his good-looking, slightly dissipated face. 'Needless to say, she despises me.'

'Heavens! Does she?'

'Unlike Kiall,' he explained, 'I've never made the grade in anything. There are only two men in Danae's life, both of them rich and powerful—Kiall and dear Daddy. Infallible giants. I simply couldn't measure up.'

'I'm sorry.' Caroline could see that he loved her.

He shrugged. 'Anyway, she's not a very nice person. And neither am I.'

Caroline glanced back into the drawing room. She didn't think Danae was a very nice person either, but she was a fabulous clothes horse. Tonight she was wearing sophisticated evening pyjamas with a plunging Vee and very little back. The colour was a bright blue, like her eyes, and she was clutching Kiall's white-jacketed arm.

'I must say they look a lovely couple. Funny how the filthy rich stick together.'

'Maybe they just like each other,' Caroline said calmly, when inside she felt anything but calm.

Joyce came to the french doors, looked around and called her. 'Caroline!'

'Don't jump.' Colin Rayment dropped a heavy hand on Caroline's arm.

'Nothing like that.' Caroline pulled away. Colin Rayment, she suspected, could quickly turn nasty.

'Ah, there you are!' Joyce exclaimed, having noted that detaining arm.

She wasn't the only one. As Kiall came towards them, Caroline guessed the reason for the narrowed eyes, the cynical twist to his calculated smile.

Extraordinarily Colin Rayment stood up and curled a serpentine arm around Caroline's tiny waist.

'Good evening,' he drawled, almost insinuatingly.

'You here, Colin?' said Danae very rudely.

'My dear, at least Joyce has a few manners.'

'How are you, Caroline?' Kiall put out his hand and Caroline took it without hesitation. She didn't like Colin Rayment at all.

'I was beginning to think you weren't coming,' she said.

'Business, dear,' Danae trilled, 'It goes on all the time.' Though she still kept a smile on her face something was disturbing her.

'Doesn't she look beautiful?' Joyce exclaimed, flashing a proud glance at Caroline.

'Unrecognisable, I'd say.' Danae raised an eyebrow.

'No, a little polished, that's all.' Kiall too was looking at Caroline, a certain hardness to his expression.

Joyce feigned to hear the undertones. 'Well, now you're here,' she said briskly, 'we can start supper.'

'Right, shall we go in, then?' Colin Rayment gave Danae a challenging stare.

'We'll be with you in a moment,' Kiall nodded towards Joyce. 'I want to have a few words with Caroline.'

Danae just barely controlled herself.

'Coming, dear?' Colin Rayment asked nastily.

It probably killed Danae to do it, but she managed a cutting: 'Of course.'

'They don't like one another, do they?' Caroline said wryly, as they moved away.

'Whether they do or they don't quite frankly doesn't interest me,' shrugged Kiall.

'You don't have a jealous streak?' From the look on his face she expected to be snubbed.

'How the devil did he manage to get an arm around you?'

Her heart was fluttering at his silver glance. 'I'm just praying he won't do it again.'

'I'll see to that!' he snapped.

'I'm not a baby.'

'I know.' He exuded male arrogance, looking down his straight nose at her.

'What did you want to talk to me about?' she asked nervously.

His hand came out, plucked a sweetly scented gardenia, then thrust it gently behind her ear. 'It suits you.' His eyes were strangely sensual and she gave a little helpless moan.

'Tell me!' she begged.

'When I told Joyce I had no objection to your staying with her, I didn't mean forever.'

'Why don't you tell me to go tonight?' She pulled her gardenia from her hair and threw it in the garden.

'I'd like to.'

'You're absolutely heartless, aren't you?' she said.

'From the day I was born.'

'People aren't talking.' She put out a pleading hand.

'Are you sure of that?'

'So what?' She had to acknowledge the number of people who were hovering curiously near the doorways. It was what they had been waiting for—Kiall's arrival, his reactions.

'So you see, it begins,' he drawled, 'The talk.'

Suddenly her nerves were raw. 'Is she, after all, one of them—a Stirling? That's what you're really frightened of, isn't it?'

'*Shut up,*' he said very quietly and distinctly, his white teeth snapping. 'My fear is for what it's going to do to both of us. People have only to see us together and all the gossip will start again.'

'Why worry about it?' she cried, scared of it herself.

'What else can I do?' His handsome face looked grim. 'The worst part is, it all seems unfinished.'

'Don't send me away, Kiall,' she pleaded.

His face tightened into a copper mask. 'I knew the moment I laid eyes on you, you'd tangle up my life.'

'I swear I'll keep out of your way.' She was now very pale, staring up at him, and there were tears in her eyes.

'Don't cry,' he said, as though his instinctive desire was to hit her.

'I don't think I can stop myself.'

He saw the genuine distress on her face and put a hard, warning hand on her bare shoulder. 'I'll give you everything you want, if you'll go away,' he told her.

'All I've ever wanted is a little love.' Her body was trembling uncontrollably at his touch.

'Any number of poor fools can give you that.'

'Well, darlings?' Joyce intervened at that moment out of sheer perceptiveness. 'Good God,' she hissed at Kiall, as she drew closer, 'you're making the child cry!'

'Not at all, Joyce. I loathe tears, as you well know.'

'I'm *not* crying!' Caroline flashed him a glittering, emerald look. 'I was actually telling Mr Stirling, I'm a perfectly free agent.'

'With anyone else but Kiall,' Joyce said dryly, 'it would do the trick. Might I remind you, my darlings, of the overwhelming interest issuing this way.'

'Don't worry, Joyce,' Kiall said smoothly, 'I've said my little piece.'

'And as far as I'm concerned, 'Caroline said scathingly, 'it fell on barren ground.'

The rest of the night passed in a waking nightmare. Only Joyce's great talent as a hostess overrode it all. Danae and Colin spent their time directing venomous barbs from one to the other and belatedly Caroline began to play the incipient femme fatale. It was altogether a stylish performance, and for the last few hours of the party she was surrounded on all sides.

'I wouldn't dream of giving another one,' Joyce said later.

A few days later Thea Stirling saw Caroline in the town, but she gave no sign, rushing past Caroline's momentarily frozen figure into a chauffeur-driven Daimler.

How she hates me, Caroline thought. She even looked a little mad. But something had been unleashed on the town; she felt it herself, the pulsing air, the conversations that seemed to stop as she passed by. Nevertheless she was determined to stick it out. She had been a refugee all her life, now nothing and no one was going to drive her out.

Inevitably the farmhouse drew her back. On the afternoon Joyce had her friends over to play bridge Caroline found herself heading towards the farmhouse. There had been no problem getting her driver's licence, and the little Japanese car she and Joyce had picked out she managed without the slightest difficulty.

Even in the passage of a few weeks the property had a disturbingly haunted air. Lizards flicked through the cracks in the timber floor of the verandah and even the front door seemed to resist Caroline's entry. All the fears she was fighting to keep buried strained to the surface.

In the hallway she stared in the blemished mirror above the old Victorian credenza, suddenly unhappy with herself, unhappy with what she was trying to do. Stay on when she wasn't wanted. Maybe there was no resting place for her anywhere.

The sudden rumble of thunder made her whip around in a panic and she walked out on to the verandah again, looking up at the sky. It was blindingly blue except for livid clouds over the highest peaks of the granite massifs. It was mid-December and the hazards of the Wet were upon them. It had rained the night before and the smothered earth and vines were alight with the brilliant tropical butterflies. Joyce had pointed out the varieties; the birdwings and the lacewings, the spotted triangles and cruisers, the magnificent Ulysses with its uppersides the most gorgeous, iridescent blue. The lantana was a maze of brilliant colour and beating wings. The parrots too were in flight, darting from one nectar-filled blossom to the other, a swirl of dazzling colour, and all the while a black snake stayed in invisible position under the front stairs.

It was all very beautiful, very wild. She sat down in the planter's chair she had painted yellow and began to brood on her troubles. Those grape-coloured clouds on the horizon seemed to magnify her sense of foreboding, as if to say; Nothing, foolish Caroline, is gentle up here.

A beautiful parrot flew at a crazy angle right on to the verandah, strutting saucily towards her, its brilliant yellow and lime green head cocked to one side.

'Aren't you gorgeous!' Caroline murmured in her sweetest voice. It was impossible to mistake its overture of friendship. She laughed aloud because it made her feel happy, but she disturbed the bird and it immediately streaked off to the safety of the laden magnolia.

Much as she cherished Joyce's friendship, she would have liked to come back and live at the farmhouse, listen to the butterflies beat their velvet wings. She supposed in that respect she was a little strange, but she had always been used to her own company. There were only two things she was good at really: studying and being alone.

All the time, the sky was changing; the livid area growing, with arrows of lightning aimed at the forest clad peaks. The foreground, however, was still the same incredible deep blue, an ecstatic colour like the sea. It would be wise not to leave it too late to get back to Joyce. Ten minutes later, when she was shaking the dust out of the old books in the tall bookcase, a voice from the verandah startled her; a coldly precise voice and one she remembered well.

'May I come in? The door was open.'

Before Caroline could say a word either way, Thea Stirling had passed through the front door, a formidable lady in a grey silk dress.

In the heat, Caroline found herself shivering slightly. 'Tell me, Miss Stirling, how did you know I was here?' she asked.

'Simple, my dear.' Thea Stirling sat down, an expression of distaste on her pale, imperious face. Not for her a sun tan. 'I followed you.'

'For what reason?'

Miss Stirling shrugged this aside as unworthy. 'You

know very well.' She gestured towards the armchair opposite her. 'Sit down.'

'An order?' Caroline made no attempt to obey.

'As you like.' Miss Stirling found a cushion and propped it behind her back. 'Kiall asked me to come and speak to you.'

'About what?'

The woman stared at her fixedly for a moment. 'Have you decided to go away?'

'I told you, I have no place to go.'

'Perhaps it would help if I wrote you a cheque?' Miss Stirling drew her leather handbag on to her lap. 'I can't decide if you're a little fool or incredibly cunning.'

'I don't fit either of those descriptions.' Caroline looked at the beautiful pearls around this terrible woman's throat. 'What about the pearls? They look real.'

Instantly the contemptuous light eyes flashed over her, alight with triumph. 'They're worth a great deal.'

'So apparently is my disappearance,' observed Caroline coldly.

'So we understand one another?'

'I understand you want me gone.'

'Don't you realise if you stay, there's danger?'

Caroline recoiled from that furious tone. 'Danger? From whom?'

'You *must* go away,' Thea Stirling repeated. 'I won't have you here!'

Caroline was struggling to make sense of the woman's tension and dread. 'But surely I can't hurt you. You have a leading position in this town. I have nothing. What is it you fear? A secret laid bare? Do you really think I could be your brother's child?'

Thea Stirling seemed beyond shock or surprise.

'You *must* go,' she said rigidly.

'But you could be my aunt! Could you really hate me?'

'Yes.' The strange light eyes raked Caroline's face. 'All I can see in you is your mother.'

'And that's so bad?' Caroline's legs were shaking badly, but still she did not sit down.

'I hated her too,' said Thea bitterly.

'You've got it down to an art.' Caroline felt her reserves of strength were running out. 'Do you know something you're not telling me?'

'What really brought you here?' Thea Stirling challenged.

'The house originally. Now I find it very beautiful.'

'I think someone put you up to it,' Thea Stirling said. 'And so does Kiall. I understand. You told me yourself. You've had nothing all your life, now you're hoping for a fortune to be settled on you.'

'You never did tell me how much!' Now Caroline was really angry. Money—that was all this woman truly valued in her heart. Money. Position. No breath of scandal.

'Fifty thousand.'

'Not enough.'

There was no quivering of Thea Stirling's thin lips, just a rigid control. 'You seem more like your mother than ever. She was a little opportunist—followed Martin all the way out from England. No family, you know, no money to speak of. He actually picked her up, paid her way out. I recognised her for what she was at once.'

'You lied to your brother too,' Caroline said bleakly, seeing how it might have been.

'And if I did?' Miss Stirling showed no remorse. 'The relationship had to be ended for the good of both of them. She wasn't good enough for my brother in any way, just a silly, soft-spoken little blonde. He could have had any girl he wanted, the daughters of any of our friends, instead he lost his head over a designing little witch.'

'I know she wasn't any of those things,' Caroline said with calm certainty. 'I know too you must have a lot on your conscience.'

'How dare you!' Thea Stirling's face went bloodless. 'How *dare* you accuse me of anything! I adored my brother.'

'Love can be every bit as destructive as hate. You must have used Edward Marshall as your pawn.'

Thea Stirling nodded. 'I wasn't ashamed of it. I knew how he felt about Deborah. He wanted her at any price.'

'And how we've all paid!' Caroline felt her locket, cold against her breast. 'You acted wickedly, and you know it.'

'At least you don't lack courage,' Thea Stirling gave her a terrible smile. 'There is no real proof who your father was. You *could* be my brother's child, but never, ever, could I accept you as my niece. You have nothing of my brother in you.'

'Just so long as I haven't inherited anything of you!' Caroline returned tartly. 'You're a real drop of poison.'

Thea Stirling stood up. 'Young people! No breeding, no respect for their elders.'

'Small wonder!' Caroline drew a ragged breath. That she had been so rude was causing her distress, but considering Miss Stirling's brutal niceness she felt she was behaving better than most. The gentlest people did strange things when provoked. Sister Lucy had slapped one girl who had driven her around the bend.

Thea Stirling lingered by the doorway, a certain greyness in her face. 'I know your kind. You know that.'

'You don't know me at all.' Caroline walked slowly towards the door, a dignity in her every movement. 'I'm not a stray you can whip out of town. I'm a person.'

'Apparently,' the older woman sneered. 'I guess I'll just have to try something else after all.'

'I'd be interested to know what?' Young as she was, Caroline was clearly not shattered by the implied threat.

'You're not the only one who can play games, my dear.' The sneering smile broadened. 'By the time I'm finished with you, you'll give anything to be able to walk out of town.'

'Good luck.' Caroline looked straight at her. 'But don't confide in Kiall. He won't like it.'

Thea Stirling threw up her hand sharply and struck Caroline's face. 'I'll take my chances with my own nephew. Don't think he'd be taken in by a little fool like you. He doesn't want you here either.'

Caroline's cheek was stinging savagely, but she didn't touch it. 'If he's afraid of me,' she said strangely, 'it's not for the same reason.'

For just an instant she thought Thea Stirling was going to strike her again, but the woman moved back, her handsome face ravaged. 'You *are* like your mother,' she whispered hoarsely.

'No,' Caroline stood closer to face her. 'Stronger. My father gave me that.'

In front of her eyes Thea Stirling seemed to crumple. She uttered a choked cry, then fled down the steps. The Daimler, Caroline could see, was parked beyond the front gate and she wondered if the chauffeur had heard their raised voices.

I can't have a worse day than this, she thought.
There was a horror in being hated, and Thea Stirling
hated her. She waited until the big silver car had pulled
away, then she walked back into the living room. A
dozen of the old leather-bound classics were still on
the table and distractedly she picked them up and put
them back into the glass-fronted bookcase. Mould had
got to some of them, which was a pity. All her favour-
ties were there; the Brontës, Jane Austen, Dickens and
Thomas Hardy, volumes of poetry, scores of books
really. One day she would go through the lot.

Her hands were shaking badly. *The Divine Comedy*.
She opened the musty old edition, reading the name
inscribed on the flyleaf: Edward Thomas Marshall. It
was a good hand, firm and full of character. Who said
one could read such things from penned words on a
page? Inwardly she despised Edward Marshall. A
photograph fell out of the book on to the polished floor
and she bent to retrieve it.

A handsome young boy and behind him, a stern-
faced woman. Nothing on the back. Caroline stared at
the old photograph, seeing the type resemblance of the
boy to the adult Martin Stirling. The resemblance
would have been more striking with each in adulthood.
Both were dark, light-eyed, though Joyce had told her,
'Teddy's eyes were blue', Both had classic, very regular
features, though the face in Caroline's locket, like Kiall
Stirling, had a cleft chin. Edward Marshall had not.
Nor did he have that certain something that trans-
cended mere handsomeness.

She put the photograph down, leafing through the
pages. Hell. Purgatory. Paradise. Many sections were
underlined. Edward Marshall had gone through his
own tortures. Caroline sighed deeply and replaced the

book. When she felt better she would do something about the dust and the mould. She loved books. Books and learning. Even when it hurt her. She looked around the room, and tears welled into her eyes. All the lonely years she had remained dry-eyed; now she was going to do her crying all at once.

She was aware of the sounds of the approaching storm, but now it didn't seem to matter. The storm matched her mood. She stroked her silver-blonde hair back from her temples, thinking she had better shut the windows in the car. It would be better if she was alone for a while. Joyce was very perceptive and she would spot her disturbed mood. Why worry Joyce? She wasn't a young woman any more, for all the wonderful way she rallied.

Now the cumulus clouds had climbed to great heights spreading out across the sky, the gun metal and the silver-grey speared with a million tints. It had all happened with such dramatic suddenness. Caroline stood there in a trance as flocks of birds, wings outstretched, homed in to safety. They knew the storm was coming and they were screeching a warning. She had never seen a sky like that. It should be painted.

Almost dazedly she wound up the windows of her little car, then drove it in under the house. There could be hail. But even then she didn't realise the terrible power of tropical storms, the element of hell.

She was scarcely inside the house when a station wagon drove up the avenue of trees. From the raised window she saw the gleaming bonnet as it slid in under the house. He must have known his aunt had been to see her. She leaned back against the bookcase, almost whispering to herself. There was no mercy from the Stirlings.

On the verandah he called her name. 'Caroline?'

She had a mad desire to lock him out, small girl cowardice, but instead she went on shaky legs to the front door.

There was dead silence for a few moments as they looked at one another, and underneath it all the ominous rumbling of the storm. The sun had gone blind behind the banked-up clouds and now the trees were waving as the wind whipped up.

Kiall broke the silence, looking as if he might lose his temper. 'For God's sake, what are you doing out here?'

'You didn't follow me?'

'Not this time.' He drew in his breath, got hold of her arm and almost shoved her inside. 'Don't you know anything about storms? Close those windows and pull the shutters.'

'What are you expecting, a tornado?'

He totally ignored her, moving with lithe efficiency about the bungalow. More to do something than placate him she followed, discovering the wind was now too strong for her to pull the wooden shutters.

'Get out of the way.' He removed her bodily, accomplishing easily what she, struggling, had failed to do. 'Can't you leave this damned place alone?'

'No.' Beside him she looked very small and defenceless.

'It's morbid,' he said angrily. 'Joyce told me you'd come here.'

'Not your dear aunt?'

'And what's that supposed to mean?' He swung on her so menacingly, she retreated a few steps.

'She's been here,' she explained.

'Thea has?' His winged brows flew together.

'She said, on your behalf.' It was gloomy now with the shutters closed, musky and claustrophobic.

His silver eyes should have slashed her to ribbons. 'I don't send women as my emissaries.'

'You don't like women at all.'

'So far I can't argue with that,' he agreed.

'What about your mother and sisters?'

'I make an exception of what belongs to me.'

'What about Danae?' A chink of light through a broken shutter held her in a spotlight; the colour of her hair and her eyes, the lightest gold veneer on her beautiful skin. She was wearing a white sundress sprigged with tiny yellow roses and green leaves and inside it her body had a ballerina's fragility.

'What about Danae?' he asked tautly.

'Aren't you going to marry her?'

'Probably. 'He gave a harsh laugh. 'What's it got to do with you anyway?'

'I can't help but think you deserve one another.'

Outside there was a great flash of lightning and a few moments after, the tumultuous crack of thunder. It startled her so much her body jumped in shock.

'How would you stand up to a cyclone?' Kiall asked derisively.

'But aren't you sending me home before one arrives?'

'Stay,' he said savagely, 'and you'll pay the price.'

The atmosphere inside the bungalow was more electric than the livid world beyond. Caroline gave a forlorn little exclamation and turned away. 'How long will the storm last?' she asked.

'I hope before it sweeps us under.' His dark face betrayed the fact that he wasn't completely under control.

She stopped talking then, sitting down on the sofa and leaning her head back. There were patches of damp on the white, plastered ceiling.

Kiall walked to the broken shutter and stared out for a while. 'What did Thea want?' he asked,

'Let's talk about it some other time.'

'No, Caroline,' he said. 'Let's talk about it now.'

'Your aunt truly hates me.' She tried to say it as calmly as she could. 'No joke, being hated.'

'She upset you?' he asked bluntly.

'We upset one another. I don't think she's entirely sure if I'm her niece or not.'

'Clever Caroline,' he said. 'You be what you want to be.'

'Your cousin?' Why was she provoking him?—and she was, without question.

'We've already settled that. Do you think I wouldn't know?'

'How?' she challenged him, her green eyes on fire.

'Because you're not my cousin. You couldn't be.'

'Unthinkable, really, for a Stirling, an illegitimate relative,' she agreed coldly.

He didn't answer, but his face tightened alarmingly. He couldn't cure himself or her with more concrete denials.

'It makes a difference, doesn't it?' she said quietly. 'What do you really see for me, Kiall?'

'You're a beautiful girl. You've got everything going for you. But not here.'

The wind seemed a thousand times stronger now, or was it consistent with the emotions within? In due course, the rain; crashing on the iron roof so the noise was deafening. Fear-maddened, Caroline slumped her head and put her hands over her ears. She refused to believe there could be such violence. When the lightning flashed it illuminated the darkened room, an eerie glow that went with the smell of sulphur.

From the livid green in the black nimbus clouds

hail was born. It descended with the dangerous wind and while Caroline writhed around at the terrifying noise the unprotected windows at the side of the house blew in.

'Stay there!' Kiall warned her as she jumped to her feet.

The metallic explosions on the roof as the hail hit assaulted her ears while in the garden a big fig tree was blown to splinters. Another sharp crack and her knees buckled under her. The lightning outside the exposed window was violet, chain lightning that could kill.

When the broken shutter blew out, she ran to it, recoiling as the force of the wind blew her back. The garden was bathed in a peculiar light, lashed by rain, hailstones like a brilliant display of diamonds all over the lawn.

'Kiall!' she called in a panic.

Even as she called the glass cracked, the shattered fragments missing her by a fraction. All but one. A diamond triangle lodged in the tender skin below her collarbone and a trickle of blood ran down on to her dress.

'Are you hurt?' He caught her from behind, turning her quickly in his arms.

'No,' she quavered. 'A piece of glass.'

'Don't faint,' he said sternly, warned by her pallor.

She blinked her eyelashes and looked away, willing the sickness inside her to subside.

More gently than she could ever have thought possible, he removed the glass, holding her firmly by the arm while he led her to the bathroom. The medicine cabinet was just as she had left it—soap, talcum powder, toothpaste, tissues, a glass jar full of fluffy cotton wool balls. No antiseptic.

'It just pricked you, that's all.' He pushed the shoestring strap off her shoulder and dabbed at the tiny wound with a damp tissue. A spot of blood welled up again and he held his finger there, exerting a little pressure.

Caroline couldn't say anything, but looked at his lean brown fingers near her breast. It was like spinning in the eye of a storm, flesh on flesh. He too was silent, standing tall and motionless by her side. If he took her hand he could feel her pulse, the fire that ran through her at his touch.

Stop it, she thought. *Stop it!*

Outside the storm was mighty, but the forces seemed more stupendous inside. It took all her strength not to lean her weary head against his chest. Of course he had enraptured her—something that would bring the wrath of heaven down upon her head.

'Let's go, baby,' he said gently. 'Back into the other room. The storm will soon be over.'

Once, long ago, her mother had been in love with Martin Stirling. And they both died. So many people who had never got over it: Kiall, Thea, Edward Marshall. The town. Profane love.

Ten minutes and the storm had reached its climax. Caroline watched as Kiall opened back the shutters, then a window, letting in a freshening blast of air and the smell of rain to the overheated room. The great clouds had lifted a little, exposing a golden ray of the sun.

'The fig tree is over,' he said quietly, stooping his wide shoulders so he could see out.

She joined him at the window as though impelled by an unseen force. The rush of fragrant wind lifted her hair, skeining it out in a gilded cloud. A thick strand caught on his damp shirt and he half turned, looking down at it with a curious expression on his hard, handsome face.

Just a breath of space was between them and, forgetting all pride, she turned up her face.

He pulled her to him almost violently, pressing his mouth down on hers, so punishingly at first, he hurt her. Then when she murmured incoherently, the cruel pressure lessened and he moved his mouth down the satin skin of her throat and back to her mouth, the source of all sweetness.

How was it, though she was small, her body perfectly fitted his own?

'I could do anything to you, couldn't I?' His lean, long-fingered hand moved over her young breast, teasing the nipple, and the spurt of excitement made her desperate and dizzy. She pressed even closer to his warm, hard body, overcome by sensations too tumultuous for her to handle. There was no reality at all, but flesh that burned where they touched.

'Witch!' he muttered harshly.

She sensed the danger in him, the passion and the supercharged hostility. What he was feeling was completely primitive, but she didn't care. It was a woman's nature to yield; man's to take.

Now the sun was out, shatteringly brilliant, and he lifted her and carried her away from the window. When he kissed her again it was worse than ever, whirling her away into the glittering world of the senses. Too fast. She began trembling quite uncontrollably, his mouth on hers, his hands cupping her naked breasts. She never knew it was possible to be so intensely aware of sensation, the excruciating pleasure.

The scent of his skin was in her nostrils; the brush of his black brows and eyelashes against her sensitive skin. Terror lay in such pleasure. The loss of self.

Nerve ends too close to the surface. The excitement was unbearable.

'Please, Kiall . . . no!'

Her eyes were tightly closed and he folded her against his chest. 'Why do you deserve such kindness?'

Her heartbeat had to slow. She hadn't breath enough left to answer.

'Rest, little one,' he said in a drained voice.

'Kiall?'

'Don't talk.'

He held her until her breathing calmed, and the trembling had almost left her body. Nothing in the world would have been easier than to stay there for ever, Caroline thought. She had come to the point where there was no past, no future, just herself pressed against his heart. A time for memory. Her richest, saddest moments. Whatever he felt for her was neither love nor pity, but a desperate physical passion, something that meant no more to him than food or drink. It was she who needed him, she who was deeply committed and afraid of the terrible consequences.

She felt his hands on the bodice of her dress, straightening the thin straps, and another racking shudder passed through her body. 'I think the storm made me a little mad,' she said shakily.

'Madness, yes,' he said with an odd, blind anger. 'To stand within a foot of each other is to invite that.'

'If you want me to,' she said painfully, 'I'll go away.'

'You'd be safe.' His hand closed under her chin. 'I might not be able to stop myself next time.'

'And you want to stop, don't you?'

'Yes.' He was cruel in the face of her misery.

Somehow she was on her feet, half running to the door. The moist breeze flowed over her as she pulled open the door and rushed out on to the verandah. It was astonishing the havoc the storm had wrought.

She heard Kiall call her name quite urgently and in a sudden shock of revulsion she saw the snake. She tried to scream but only succeeded in giving a choking gasp. She was on it as it slid from the shelter of the verandah.

Kiall leapt for her, moving with incredible swiftness, but he was no match for the snake. Disturbed, it struck within seconds, rearing up and releasing its venom into Caroline's leg. She staggered and Kiall's hand bore down with ruthless power, seizing the snake and smashing its head against the heavy wooden pillar. His dark face was savage and his breath hissed through his clamped teeth.

'*Caroline!*' On one knee he swooped over her, gripping her leg above the puncture marks.

A dreadful, weak little laugh gushed out of her. 'You might be free of me sooner than you think.'

His glittering eyes met her own, but he did not speak. With one hand he whipped off his belt, the other still holding her leg, but what followed Caroline was never to remember. Giving in to a vast sickness, she fell heavily unconscious.

CHAPTER EIGHT

A SOUND jolted Caroline awake.

Impossible, she thought; I'm in a hospital. She began to weep; weak tears that slid out of her eyes on to the white pillow.

'Now, now!' A nurse plunged through the door, all hale and hearty. 'We're awake!'

'Regrettably.' Almost instantly Caroline regained her self-possession.

'Naughty!' the cheery face regarded Caroline very closely. 'You're a lucky girl.'

'What makes you say that?'

'Dearie, you were practically at death's door. I mean, putting your foot in a snake's mouth!'

'I didn't see it,' Caroline returned ironically.

'Goodness!' the young nurse looked confused. 'Anyway, it was marvellous, Mr Stirling being on hand and all. Fancy if you'd been lying there all day!'

'I rather imagine I'd be dead.'

The nurse smiled indulgently and gave Caroline's arm a pat. 'All's well that ends well, I say.'

'Shouldn't you be more positive as a nurse?'

Nurse McInnes let that pass. 'Doctor will be here in a few moments,' she said comfortingly. 'He's doing the grand tour at the moment.'

There was nothing for it but to go back to sleep again. Caroline shut her eyes, thinking her mood must be influenced by the venom in her bloodstream.

Doctor Shepard came in on a wave of wellbeing,

pointing out again the tremendous element of luck.

'Keep it for your memoirs!' he chortled. 'You're doing nicely, but just to be on the safe side we'll keep you in another day.'

He had scarcely gone when the phone rang. It was Joyce, sounding very nearly tearful.

'My dear little girl, I was shocked!'

'I'm all right now.' Caroline was really appallingly lethargic in mind and body.

'Thank God they had the antidote. Imagine if there hadn't been a drop of it left?'

'Thanks, Joyce.' For the first time Caroline smiled.

'I shall be up this afternoon,' Joyce promised. 'Absolutely without fail.' Taking it for granted her presence was indispensable.

Which, Caroline concluded, it was. She made not the slightest attempt to eat her lunch, but when Joyce sailed in, with Paddy a little tipsy reeling after, she made a real effort to greet them in a normal manner.

Joyce conferred on her a kiss, after which Paddy slumped over. 'Gee, love, you look rotten!'

'Is that any way to talk?' Joyce rounded on him with extreme annoyance.

'I can't bear to see the kid look so bloody tragic!'

Joyce was thinking the same thing. 'Be a good man,' she said firmly to Paddy, 'and step aside.'

'You can 'ave the chair, Joycie.' Paddy settled her into it, used to being ticked off.

'There's one outside the door,' Joyce told him levelly. 'Go and get it.'

'I feel as if I've known you for ever,' Caroline said, looking into Joyce's concerned face.

'You're supposed to.' Joyce patted her arm. 'Tell me how it happened. Kiall rang me, of course, but I greatly fear he was upset. That is to say, he told me practically nothing.'

'Saved your life,' Paddy nodded, his head to one side. 'You really ought to know you don't tread on snakes.'

'Really, Paddy!' Joyce sighed. 'You're the ideal sick-room visitor!'

'Someone's got to tell 'er!'

'Life in the jungle,' Caroline said, the glitter of tears in her eyes.

Joyce gave her a look of concern. 'Everything is going to be all right now,' she exclaimed. 'I've got a little holiday lined up.'

'You're much too good to me, Joyce,' protested Caroline.

'Where are you goin'?' Paddy asked, trying to match Joyce's attempt at lightheartedness.

'Over to one of the islands for a few days,' Joyce decided briskly. 'Caroline will love it.'

Seeing she was tiring, they didn't stay beyond twenty minutes. They stared at her with frank amazement when she told them she simply hadn't seen the snake on the verandah, and if they concluded she must have had something very pressing on her mind, they made no mention of it. Neither did Caroline tell them Thea Stirling had visited her. She would tell Joyce when they were alone. For all Paddy's goodhearted-ness, he was solidly behind the Stirlings.

Doctor Shepard called again, speaking quite rever-ently of Kiall. Probably he was in the habit of donating trifling sums to the hospital. Trifling for *him*, Caroline thought. Sensing her lack of interest, the good doctor trailed off. Odd, really, he thought, when Stirling had saved the girl's life. No question about it, quick thinking plus the right antidote and a stark tragedy had been averted.

The day droned on into dusk. Caroline dozed fitfully. She wanted to keep her mind a blank, but it was difficult. She kept hearing Kiall call her name; the fear and the urgency. It had been a miracle he had been there. Though if she hadn't been so distraught she would never have rushed out on to the verandah like a mad thing. He would have realised that. In the moments before unconsciousness she had recognised his profound fear.

When the thought of him got too much, she sat up, pushed the bedclothes back and swung her legs out of bed. Her injured leg felt stiff and she started to move her toes, staring downwards so her hair cascaded to one side and curtained her face.

'What do you think you're doing?' a voice asked grimly. Kiall strode to the bedside, his glance brilliant with near-anger. 'You have to take it quietly.'

'Oh, I'd love to!' She gave an unsettled little laugh.

'Lie back.' He put his hand on her shoulder and pressed her back against the pillows.

'Don't you wish they couldn't find the antidote?' Her body was trembling under its thin covering.

'Stop it, Caroline,' he said tersely. 'How do you feel?'

'Battered. Broken. Bruised.' She said it flippantly, but that was exactly how she felt.

'You're just nervy.' He pulled the chair around and sat down in it, the lines from nostril to firm mouth more pronounced.

'I suppose I should thank you for saving my life,' she said flatly.

'I'd rather you didn't.'

'That's straight enough, anyway.'

He ignored her, more austere than she had ever seen him. 'I've spoken to Shepard. He said you could go home in the morning.'

She gave a little bitter laugh. 'Home? Where exactly is that?'

He bent his raven head, but she saw the muscle jerk beside his mouth. 'What happened was pretty terrible for both of us, Caroline.'

'Meaning what? Were you concerned?'

'I can't recall too many worse moments,' he said crisply.

'But you weren't to blame.' Her eyes were as brilliant as his.

'If you didn't look so frail,' he said tautly, 'I'd shake you.'

'But then you're a violent man.'

'Sometimes. With you.' He glanced at her pale face, then away again, through the open door. 'Odd, that, when you need the gentlest handling.'

Caroline drew in her bottom lip and bit it hard. Everything about him hurt her, the look and the sound, the tautness that was in his lean body. If he weren't so hard, so supremely arrogant, she would have thought him deeply upset.

'And how did your aunt take the news?' she asked. 'Sorry, I'll bet!'

'I've spoken to her,' he returned curtly.

She flushed at his tone, and lay back against the pillows, fragile enough to be breakable. 'As a matter of interest, what did she say?'

'All that matters now is that you get better.'

'No answer at all.' She realised with sudden shame that she was desperate for him to hold her, aching for the stimulation of his touch. He was so vivid, so vital. A single touch could heal her.

'Lie quietly.' He put his hand on her shoulder and blindly, without willing it, she turned her cheek so it nuzzled against his hand.

'*God!*' Kiall drew in his breath sharply.

'Pathetic, aren't I?' she said weakly.

'What if I do what you want? What then?' He was furiously angry, his eyes narrowed to slits.

Humiliated, Caroline turned away, so all he could see was the poignant line of her profile. 'You turned me into a woman, Kiall. Now you want to forget it.'

The handsome mouth quirked in derision. 'Aren't you being melodramatic? You were born a seductress.'

'And you so hate yourself for noticing!'

'I'm like that.' He stood up restlessly, tension in every line of his lean, powerful body. 'I don't mean to hurt you, Caroline.'

'Oh yes, you do. You take a pride in it.' Her voice was muffled up in pain. 'I suppose it's a kind of revenge.'

'Maybe,' he said with hard cynicism. 'Nothing good is built on ruins.' His eyes struck grimly on her face and the relaxed line of her body.

'You're appallingly cruel,' she said shakily.

'Don't I have to be?' he countered.

'We couldn't possibly be related by blood.'

Instead of agreeing he went rather white. 'The best thing I can do is cut short this visit.'

Caroline turned back to him and there were tears in her eyes. 'And I want you to go. Thank you for saving my life—much as it went against the grain.'

For a moment he stood motionless, staring down at her, then he swung around and walked out of the room.

For almost a week Caroline recuperated in the magic of a coral island. Physically she was much better, responding to the beauty around her, the glorious blue of the sky and the crystal clear water. Joyce kept her moving—swimming, daily walks around the island, hunting shells, visiting the other islands in the launch, losing herself in the fantastic world of the coral gardens; anything and everything that made her eat and sleep better. On the Reef it was all peace and glorious scenery. Even the weather held, though on the day the launch came for them to take them back to the mainland there was a cyclone watch on a low in the Coral Sea.

Joyce was as tanned as a Red Indian, but she had made sure Caroline, with her very fair skin, kept much of the time under cover. So Caroline's face and her straight slender limbs had only the palest gold colour.

'Can't risk skin cancer, m'dear!'

Caroline often asked why Joyce was lying prone in a tropical sun, and Joyce always replied that she was a sun-worshipper. Besides, she had an olive skin and dark eyes.

By the time they arrived home it was raining hard and there were gale warnings all along the coast.

'Made it just in time!' Joyce announced with satisfaction. 'It's strange, but I really do think I have an influence on the weather.'

Though their friendship was of such short standing in terms of time, they were temperamentally very compatible. In fact they had a kind of allied quality which would become more marked as Caroline grew older. Without setting out to be, both had the stamp of being different.

It was during a late dinner that the phone rang and when Joyce came back, her expressive face was intrigued.

'For you, m'dear. An unfamiliar voice—male.'

'Didn't he say who he was?' Caroline folded her napkin.

'He said would it be possible to speak to Miss Caroline Marshall.'

'I'd rather not,' she protested.

'It could be an admirer!' Joyce urged. 'He sounded young and rather nice.'

'In other words, you want me to answer.' Caroline rose carefully and walked through to the entrance hall.

'Caroline Marshall,' she said rather sternly.

'Caroline,' the voice said. 'Ian Randall here.'

She couldn't have been more surprised. 'Surely you're not in Stirling?' Not a man terrified of cyclones?

'As a matter of fact I am.'

'Good lord!' Caroline pulled a face at Joyce, who had come to stand beside her. 'A holiday or what?'

'Actually I followed you.' An attractive laugh. 'Dad wanted me to see how you were getting on.'

'I'm staying with a friend,' she told him.

'Ask him over,' Joyce hissed behind her hand.

'How long are you staying, Mr Randall?' Caroline asked in the spirit of politeness.

'*Ian*, please,' he laughed again. 'I have a month in all. I'd like us to meet. What about tomorrow?'

'Take him for a drive,' said Joyce, when Caroline finally got off the phone.

'In the rain?'

'Up here we don't let the rain stop us.'

'But I don't really like him. He took me out to dinner, did you know?'

'Surely you're not going to hold that against him?' Joyce enquired. 'You're singularly without vanity, m'dear. You're a beauty.'

'I'm Deborah's daughter,' she said, with a tightness

in her chest. By my face you shall know me.

Ian made a good impression on Joyce. He was good-looking in a fair, unflappable way, well bred, well mannered and on his very best behaviour.

'What a magnificent home you have here, Miss Coddington,' he told her. 'A jewel!'

Fortunately the rain eased very slightly, for despite his attentions to Joyce, it was apparent Ian was impatient for some precious moments alone with Caroline.

Joyce came to the door to see them off, saying exactly where and where not they should go. There were numerous beauty spots and scenic drives, but certain roads would be awash, not to say impassable, after the rain.

'Nice little car,' Ian said kindly.

'Secondhand, but then it had to be,' explained Caroline.

'I'm so glad you're not at the farm.' Ian glanced appreciatively at her profile. She had changed out of all recognition since he had seen her last. Not in feature, of course, but in aura. She had ripened. A child no longer, but a very beautiful young woman. 'I went there, you know.'

'Really? I didn't want to leave it.'

'But so lonely! It looked haunted to me.'

'It is.' Caroline gave a little choking laugh.

Ian looked a bit uneasy. 'Where are you taking me?' he asked by way of diversion, when actually he didn't care.

'Would you like to go into town? Have a cup of coffee, sit down. There's so much wind it's pushing the car around.'

'Damned dangerous, isn't it?' Ian dipped his fair head to stare out at the waving trees. 'God knows how they survive.'

'Used to it,' Caroline smiled. 'Doesn't danger give a heightened sense of living?'

'Does it?' Ian frowned dubiously. 'I find this wind more frightening than exciting.'

'But it isn't anything,' Caroline pointed out slyly, though her small hands were white on the wheel. 'Wait for the big blow.'

'I should think the whole place would come down like a pack of cards!'

Ten minutes later they were sitting having coffee in the best of the excellent Italian coffee shops around the town. From their vantage point beside the window, they could look out at the poinciana-lined street, watching all the blossoms fall in the high wind.

'Do you think it will strike?' Ian asked almost fearfully.

'I hope not.' Caroline looked out at the wind-tossed, rain-washed sky. 'This kind of weather is not unusual for this time of the year. The locals don't take much notice until they have to. The weather men keep the watch with their radar screens and their satellite photographs. They've only issued a cyclone watch so far. We'll all be alerted in time.'

'Pleasant town,' Ian murmured, as though he saw it being swept on to the Great Barrier Reef.

'Don't worry,' Caroline said consolingly. 'The police and the civil defence team are very efficient.'

'Seems like they're working it out now!' Ian jerked a hand towards the white-timbered Colonial-style police station across the street. A uniformed inspector had come out on to the verandah, in deep conversation with a younger man who towered over him. Both wore sober, preoccupied expressions.

'Good-looking chap!' Ian said sharply. 'Who the devil is he?'

Caroline tried to look unperturbed. 'Kiall Stirling. The other man is Inspector Warren.'

'Stirling?' Another frown accompanied that information. 'Any connection with the town?'

'Just a friendly gesture. It was named after one of his illustrious forebears.'

'Good heavens!' Ian didn't seem pleased.

'It's customary enough. Even topical.' Caroline watched as Inspector Warren gave his departing visitor a crisp salute. 'A property up here, Mount Spencer, was named after Earl Spencer, and one of his kinsmen took it up. Later on it was sold to the Finch-Hatton brothers, sons of the Earl of Winchelsea. Henry, the heir, went home, but Harold stayed on, to turn into a real character. Apparently he formed a one-man separation league for North Queensland. It had a registered office in London. The town of Finch-Hatton was named after them.'

'You're very knowledgeable.' Ian seemed unable to tear his eyes away from Kiall Stirling's striding figure.

'Joyce told me.' Caroline sighed. 'There were plenty of blue-bloods out here in the early days, second sons who wanted to take up their own great selections. The Stirlings, I believe, are very well connected.'

'I see,' Ian murmured, almost angrily. 'Do you know him at all?'

'Slightly.' Caroline gave a cool smile of bitter amusement. 'He saved my life.'

That succeeded in getting Ian's full attention. 'What in the world do you mean?' He bent closer and touched her hand.

'I was bitten by a snake not so long ago. Kiall's being there happened to save my life.'

Ian's blue eyes reflected hostility and shock. 'I

gather from the way you say his name that you know him better than slightly?'

'No, not really.' Caroline bent her head so the sheen of her blonde hair fell about her face. 'He's not an easy person to know.'

'Has he a wife?' Ian was staring at her intently.

'You're very curious.' Caroline raised her green eyes.

'If you like.' He shrugged lightly. 'When a man's got that much style one expects him to have a beautiful wife.'

'He has a beautiful friend,' Caroline told him with a deep ache. 'I expect they'll get married one of these days.'

Ian seemed relieved. 'Then how did he come to save your life? Surely you were together some place?'

'It was at the farm.' Caroline's eyes glittered. 'Kiall opposed my being there in the first place.'

'What's it go to do with him?' Ian asked in a distinctly tight voice.

'Around here,' Caroline said huskily, 'he has a lot of say. You saw the Inspector give the big salute. Kiall is a V.I.P.'

'How extraordinary!' Ian leaned back in his chair, his coffee forgotten. 'What exactly does he do?'

'I don't really know,' Caroline said vaguely. 'I know he has big interests in timber, sugar, cattle, a tropical fruit plantation, real estate developing. More, I suppose. I've never actually asked.'

'But he sounds fabulously wealthy!' Ian looked dismayed.

'Yes,' Caroline nodded. 'Joyce told me.'

Ian's fair, good-looking face darkened as though his own future was at stake. 'I'd certainly like to meet him. Any chance?'

'Every chance if you ask Joyce.' Caroline's green eyes strayed down the street, but Kiall had gone.

'You still haven't told me what he was doing out at the farm.' Ian too glanced over his shoulder.

'There was a storm, and Kiall came to see if I was all right.' And he kissed me, made love to me, so I'll never be able to settle for less all my life.

'Has he an interest in you, then?' Ian leaned forward, pushing his plate away.

'Far from it,' Caroline said flatly. 'He wants me to go away.'

Ian didn't say anything for a moment, a stillness settling on him. 'That came from the heart,' he commented.

'I don't want to go.'

'Don't be silly!' The words were light but almost a censure. 'It's going to rain up here—I mean really rain. You belong in the city, not in cyclone country. I agree with our Mr Stirling, you don't belong here.'

'I want to,' she said quietly.

'For God's sake, you're not in love with him?' Ian framed the words despairingly.

'You've got it all wrong,' Caroline explained deliberately. 'A long time ago there was a tragedy up here, a tragedy that involved my mother and his uncle. They were killed in a car crash.'

Ian signalled for some more coffee. 'Tell me,' he said abruptly.

'I just did.' Caroline was conscious of the edge in his voice.

'I mean, the whole story. There had to be one.'

'And if there was,' she said moodily, 'no one seems to know it. My mother came out from England to marry Martin Stirling, but she changed her mind and married Edward Marshall.'

'Your father,' Ian corrected her as a matter of course. 'Was there nothing unusual about the car crash? Tragic, I know, but . . . out of the way?'

'They went over the side of a gorge.'

Ian's blue eyes under his fair brows became deeply thoughtful. 'I see,' he said dryly.

The young waitress came back with fresh coffee and they paused until she had gone away.

'It took me nearly eighteen years,' said Caroline, 'to find out how my mother died.'

'Monstrous!' Ian agreed. 'I understood your mother died in giving you birth.' He drew his coffee towards him and stirred it violently. 'But to die in a car with a man not your father! God in heaven!' he breathed.

'And in all that time,' Caroline smiled crookedly, 'the same old rumours.'

'Sounds like a bad dream.' Ian sipped at his hot coffee. 'That Stirling, he looks pretty tough.'

'A big, hard man,' Caroline agreed.

Ian nodded. 'I'd say the best thing you could do under the circumstances was to come back South with me. Let me be your friend.'

'Because you like me?'

'Yes.' Ian's blue eyes smouldered. 'Funny, when I saw you before, you were just a kid, but now you've grown up. It's not just a pretty dress and a dash of lipstick. You really have matured.'

'Put it down to life in the tropics,' Caroline smiled wryly.

Ian gave a little laugh. 'What I'm getting at is this, Caroline. I'm very attracted to you.'

'No!' Caroline shifted in her seat.

'Don't be afraid.' Ian placed a warm, calming hand over her own. 'I'm not about to make a claim on you. I just want the opportunity to get to know you better and for you to get to know me. I really ought to be married—God knows Mother never lets up on me! But you're the first girl in a long time to jolt me out of the old routine. Of course Dad was anxious to know how you were getting on, but I didn't have to come here personally. I did that because I want a closer relationship. Sitting in my office, I was forever thinking what you were doing up here.'

'I almost died.' Caroline was faintly trembling in reaction. She didn't want Ian's attention.

'It could happen again.' Ian clutched at her bare arm, firmly at first, then frankly caressing. 'The Far North is something else again. You could never regard it as home. Come back with me. We'll put the farmhouse on the market and head back to civilisation.'

'I don't know,' she sighed.

'What is it, then?' Ian was staring into her small, uncertain face. 'You only need half an eye to see that Stirling is a man who gets what he wants. And if he doesn't want you here, surely it's all over?'

And it couldn't matter more. Caroline was too disturbed to answer, too sick and weary of the whole situation. Just to sight Kiall for a few moments was to open up an aching wound.

When they were back on the street again, the moan of the wind had become a fierce howl.

'Good grief!' Ian looked up in a sudden panic. 'I think we'd better call off our sightseeing, don't you?' He kept Caroline tightly pressed to him as though the wind was going to sweep them apart.

'Come back to the house, then.' Joyce had told her to be sure to ask.

'I'd like that.' Ian hurried her on to the shelter of the car. 'Miss Coddington did invite me for a meal.'

Ian didn't offer to take the wheel and Caroline didn't

ask him, though now the rain was starting to lash down and the visibility lessen. Steam rose from the heated earth and roadways creating clouds of vapour and sections of the road were like glass.

'Turn your lights on,' Ian ordered nervously.

'They *are* on,' Caroline reproached him.

'Wouldn't it be better if you pulled over? The visibility is virtually nil.'

'Pull over where?' she asked shortly. 'I don't fancy running into the cane.'

There was nothing more said between them until they came to the crossroads.

'This place is a disaster, isn't it?' Ian looked out at the turbulent world.

'I have more pressing things on my mind.' It seemed she had to really grip the wheel to hold the little car straight. Surely Ian should have offered to drive? She knew Kiall wouldn't have cared to leave her at the wheel.

'Hell!' Ian called out so loudly, Caroline slammed on the brake.

'What's the matter?' She was icy with dismay.

'Are they toads all over the road?'

She could have wept with relief. 'The way you screeched I at least expected a crocodile!'

'But they're *enormous*!' Ian faltered.

'The cane is full of them.'

'They look so aggressive!'

Despite the tension of trying to drive in the pouring rain, Caroline had to laugh. 'It's obvious you're a townie.'

'Thank God!' Ian shuddered. 'I knew they had to burn off to get rid of the snakes, but I suppose it's really alive with vermin.'

'Any and everything that can bite and sting. Great

poisonous spiders.'

'This simply isn't my scene.' Ian was breathing shallowly.

A succession of cars was bearing down on them from the opposite direction, the last of them right over the centre line.

'What the hell is he doing?' Ian straightened up stiffly, the adrenalin quickening.

'*She,*' Caroline corrected grimly, seeing the other woman's expression—a frightened rabbit just waiting to be hit.

'Pull left!' Ian shouted with genuine panic.

'I'd be a damned fool if I didn't! 'Caroline's reflexes were excellent and under other conditions they might have driven out of the situation. The wet clay on the extreme edge of the road gave way and while Caroline held her breath the front wheel slid farther along the ridge, then down into a storm water channel.

'Hell!' Ian was struggling furiously with his seat belt.

'We're stuck, right?'

'In the pouring rain!' Ian looked off towards the canefields as though expecting King Kong to emerge. 'Don't tell me she's keeping on going?'

'Looks like it.' Caroline looked in her rear vision laconically. 'Maybe she's going for the Lone Ranger.'

'No question about women drivers!' Ian said caustically.

'You want to take over?' She looked at him.

'Who's going to get us out of here?'

Caroline felt utterly fatalistic. 'Maybe we can railroad it back into town.'

Humour under such circumstances didn't come easily to Ian. 'We'd better flag down a passing car.'

'It'd be better if we had a flag.'

Ian didn't laugh. 'I've never experienced anything so violent in my whole life. Will you just look at that storm water? If I got out it would sweep me off my feet.'

'I don't think so,' she shrugged.

'You mean you want me to?' Ian looked, of a sudden, deeply disappointed in her.

'No, that's okay. A car's coming anyway.'

'Let's hope someone responsible.' Ian tried to stare through the fogged-up rear window.

As the big car drew nearer, Caroline took a calming breath. 'The last thing you might want to do right now is meet Kiall Stirling, but you're going to.'

'Good grief!' Now Ian put a protective arm around Caroline's shoulders.

The big station wagon moved ahead of them and pulled up just left of the road, leaving on its hazard warning lights. Kiall stood out wearing a rain coat but bare headed, staring back at the precariously angled car.

'Does he usually look so formidable?' Ian asked.

Caroline didn't answer; she was winding down her window.

'Who's this?' Kiall bent his glistening black head.

'Ian Randall,' Ian shouted above the drumming on the car roof. 'Sorry to be such a terrible nuisance.'

Kiall didn't even ask what happened. 'You'll live a damn sight longer if you stay off the roads when the weather's worsening.'

'Sorry about that,' Ian apologised again, clearly not cut out to be a fearless hero.

'Let's see if you can jump out,' Kiall said briskly.

'Not this side, old man!' Ian glanced down slantways at the swiftly running water.

Kiall transferred his silvery gaze to Caroline.

'Haven't you got any protection?'

'I know where I left an umbrella.'

'Wind up your window,' he said crisply, 'and get out. Bring your keys.'

Beside her, Ian looked as if he was praying, rivulets of sweat running down his flushed face.

'Here goes!' Caroline's hand went to his shoulder consolingly, then she took a deep breath and got out of the little car as quickly as she could.

'Get under here, dammit!' Kiall snapped at her. He pulled one side of his coat away and the next thing she was smothered in its waterproof folds.

Ian wasn't accorded the same attention, and by the time he too, was safely escorted to the station wagon he was cursing quietly under his breath.

Kiall ignored him, starting up the big car and swinging it out on to the road. He went straight to Joyce's with Caroline silent, and Ian hunched wet and miserable in the back seat.

'Out! Out!' Joyce urged when she saw them.

It was wonderful to be in the solid security of the house. Caroline shook back her wet hair. 'Some silly woman nearly ran us off the road,' she told Joyce.

'Who'd be game?' Kiall asked shortly.

'She *did*!' Caroline protested. 'I want my lawyer.'

'It looks as if he's soaking wet.' Joyce was looking at Ian with a mixture of sympathy and exasperation.

'I say, what am I going to do for a change of clothes?' Ian just stood there looking nonplussed.

Kiall raked him with one of his sardonic glances. 'I'm sure Joyce can rustle up something.'

Joyce fell silent, thinking. 'Not really,' she said, upon reflection. 'Not even a trouser suit.'

'Never mind. I'll run you back to your hotel.'

If anything Ian looked worse, and a little belatedly

Joyce came to his rescue. 'You'd better stay here until it's all over. I daresay we can get someone from the hotel to run your things out.'

'How kind!' Ian looked his gratitude.

'Well, come along, then,' Joyce bade him. 'It must have been a terrible experience for you.'

Kiall looked after them and gave a short laugh. 'Isn't your hero a little feckless?'

'He has other things in good measure.' Caroline made a halfhearted attempt to dry her hair with the fluffy towel Joyce had laid out for her.

'Such as?' He took the towel from her and made a much more efficient job of it.

'He's kind,' she said in a fierce little voice. 'He came all this way to see how I was.'

'How considerate!' There was a world of mockery in his tone. 'Tell me what were you talking about when you ran off the road.'

She pulled away breathlessly, her hair a golden cloud. 'What do men and women usually talk about?'

'And you're a woman?' The insolence was stunning, the light in his eyes. Like his own world, he had a look of turbulent vitality, a look that almost made Ian, in comparision, seem effete.

'Don't you want to dry your hair?' Caroline asked.

'It's all right.' He was entirely unconcerned, the crisp black waves curling closer to his head. 'And this Randall was your father's solicitor?'

'*His* father was solicitor to the late Edward Marshall.'

'Astutely answered,' he said unpleasantly. 'No doubt he's here to protect your interests.'

'I feel safer with him here,' she lied.

'Did you ask him to come?' There was arrogance in the cut of his mouth and his nostrils.

'Subconsciously, I suppose, I willed it.'

'How nice to be a witch!'

Joyce came back into the sitting room to find it electric. 'The poor boy's quite done in,' she told them.

'I'm sure you'll gladly take care of him.' Kiall turned to leave.

'Don't be like that, Kiall,' Joyce said mildly. 'He's come all this way just to see Caroline, you know.'

'Point out to him that she's seventeen years old.'

'Eighteen,' Caroline cried, aggrieved.

'I believe it's a couple of months off.' He turned on her so swiftly, and unexpectedly she fell back to stammering.

'M-March.'

'Where's my raincoat, Joyce?' asked Kiall.

'Here, dear.' Joyce hastened to be helpful. She pulled it off the stand and held it out. 'Let me help you.'

'I can manage.'

There was something oddly daunting about him, and both women stood watching him, brooding about the fact.

'Surely you don't mind if Ian stays here?' Joyce asked, almost apologetically.

'It will save you both from moping around the house.'

A rush of wind and rain and Kiall was gone.

'Do you know, I think he was annoyed about something,' Joyce stated the obvious.

CHAPTER NINE

CYCLONE Annabel crossed the coast a scant two hundred kilometres north of Stirling, bringing in its wake torrential rain and destructive winds. In the northern township of Hungerford there were two dead and six missing and more than half the houses in the town left uninhabitable.

'Surely this makes you more increasingly aware how dangerous it is for you to stay here.' Ian stood at the big bay window looking out at the blinding sheets of rain.

'You think I *should* go back with you, don't you?' Caroline came to join him, unnerved as he was by an alien environment.

'I can't leave you here.' He put his hands on her shoulders, staring down into her upturned face. 'There's nothing for you up here, and it's a misery in the rain.'

'Normally the cyclones die away in the Pacific.'

'What about Darwin?' he said. 'The greatest natural disaster we've ever had. Cyclone Tracy destroyed the town. It was Christmas too, like now.'

'People build again.' Caroline looked out towards the immense turbulence. The garden looked almost ruined, yet she knew it would blossom again.

'What's keeping you here?' Ian clutched her with possessive hands.

'Something I didn't really expect. I love it.'

'With the wind screaming and violent rain?' Ian,

who had arrived at the worst possible time, couldn't understand what was the matter with her.

'Even that.'

She said it so calmly it made him afraid. 'You're the strangest girl I've ever met,' he sighed.

'Am I?' Her green eyes were glowing, intense, but he had the terrible feeling not for him. It made him go totally out of control, so he bent his head and kissed her passionately on her parted mouth.

'Caroline,' he whispered. 'Caroline.'

She was so stunned she didn't move, then she shook her head. 'Please, Ian!'

'But I have to!' His strong arms were shaking. 'I know you're so young, so innocent, but I can wait.'

Whatever she was going to say was swallowed up by his mouth. It was devouring, taking no note of her lack of response.

'I think I love you,' he said inaudibly against her hurting mouth. 'I don't know why, but I do.' He seemed frantic when she couldn't believe it was actually happening. 'Don't be afraid of me.' He misread her shrinking. 'It's so good to have you in my arms. I've been wanting it for days.'

Caroline felt sad and angry and ridiculous all at once. How could he be kissing her so deeply, so eagerly, when she was feeling nothing but physical discomfort! Why should one man's kisses make her moan in ecstasy and another's make her sick of the whole thing? She wanted it over; the desperate mouth and the searching hand. Was there only one man who could arouse her sexuality?

'Wouldn't it be magic if we were alone somewhere?' Ian exclaimed against her cheek. 'You're perfect . . . perfect to make love to.' His mouth returned to hers, trying to urge her lips apart. 'Don't be scared.'

'I'm not!'

He laughed quietly, beneath his breath, satisfied she was. 'I want to teach you everything there is to know.'

A tall silhouette outside the window cleared her brain instantly. 'Ian, let me go!' she begged.

'What's the matter?' It was impossible to mistake her agitation.

She didn't have to answer, for the doorbell pealed through the house. Stridently, as if it had been pushed with some violence.

'I think it's Kiall,' said Caroline in odd tones.

'So?' Ian sounded violently brought down to earth.

'He saw us.'

'Okay, he saw us.' Ian's flushed face flushed deeper. 'What's so terrible about that? You'd better get this guy into perspective. He may be the big, powerful man around here, but he doesn't own you.'

While they were standing there Joyce, who had been writing letters in her room, came out calling: 'I'll get it!'

'You're white,' Ian accused her. 'My God, you're frightened of him, aren't you?'

'I'm sure I am,' Caroline answered softly.

'You just leave him to me.' Ian caught her hand and closed it against his heart. 'I won't leave this house until you come with me.'

It couldn't be going worse, and for a moment Caroline closed her eyes, saying a silent prayer that had no words.

'Kiall's here,' Joyce told them as she preceded him into the drawing room.

'Hello there!' Ian spoke so pleasantly it was obvious he didn't intend to precipitate a confrontation then.

'Good morning.' Kiall's answering voice was very

crisp and distinct. No smile, just superb composure and brilliant eyes.

Caroline flushed and bit her lip. 'How are you, Kiall?'

'Up to my neck in problems.'

'Any way we can help?' Ian asked breezily.

The handsome mouth thinned. 'You could lend a hand. Half of Hungerford has been devastated. They need all the help they can get.'

'I'm going with Kiall,' Joyce told Caroline, determination and the willingness to help in her expression. 'I've had experience of these situations before. There's plenty I can do to help the women of the town.'

'Then I'll come too,' Caroline offered without hesitation.

'No, Caroline.' Ian turned his fair head, somewhat embarrassed. 'I'd really prefer you to stay here.'

'Why?' Caroline lifted her chin sharply.

'You'd be no good with emergency duties.'

'Why ever not?' Joyce looked puzzled. 'Caroline is a very capable little gel.'

'When you've done arguing,' Kiall said sarcastically, 'I have to go.'

Caroline asked, 'What shall I wear?'

'Are you kidding?' Kiall looked at her. 'There'll be no one there to fascinate.'

Joyce shook her head. 'I'm sure she didn't mean that, dear.' Her tone softened as she looked at Caroline. 'Get your raincoat and your gumboots and a scarf for your hair. It won't be pretty, m'dear. Human suffering never is.'

'I can help, Joyce,' Caroline spoke earnestly. 'I want to.'

'Good gel!' Joyce stomped into the entrance hall to

grab her own mackintosh and gumboots.

'What about you, Randall?' Kiall asked abruptly, looking out at the dark grey sky.

'If you think I can be of any help.' Ian, who had never been called upon to display physical courage, looked momentarily shattered.

'Good. I can lend you some gear.'

Caroline was never to forget her first encounter with devastation. Half the town was destroyed and the people dazed with shock. They flew in in Kiall's private plane, landing on a section of the highway left high and dry and taking the trip into town in one of the volunteer Range Rovers.

Joyce was shocked, but she kept cool. Caroline cried.

It looked like a scene from Hell; flattened houses, strewn timber and tiles and brickwork, buckled and twisted iron roofs, furniture that had flown through the air. Power lines were down, crackling and hissing, and above the flood waters fountains gushed from the burst mains.

Yet the people waved as they drove straight in.

'Indomitable!' said Joyce, her prominent jaw working.

'Here.' Kiall passed Caroline his handkerchief, looking as though he was cursing himself for bringing her.

Quickly she wiped away the tears.

'Keep it,' he said, 'You might need it.'

She didn't say anything, but just turned her head and looked at him, and a flicker of involuntary amusement crossed his face.

At the civic centre, Joyce proved herself equal to anything. In no time at all she had a band of women organised to cut sandwiches and make tea, and Caroline, because she was good with children, was set to finding ways of keeping them quiet and entertained.

Still it was bedlam until people satisfied themselves that their loved ones were safe. Wrecked houses could be replaced; a human life, never. There were sounds of weeping; cries of joy. Caroline did everything she could to reassure the children, but because the numbers were too great to offer personal comfort, she called out to two bruised and shaken young teenage girls who were huddling by the door:

'Please help me.' With a bawling baby on her hip and a two-year-old clinging to her skirt she needed it.

The girls were sisters, in a silent frenzy of fear because although their father's utility truck had been located there was still no trace of him.

Fifteen minutes later he walked into the emergency centre, badly cut about the head by flying debris, but miraculously alive.

'Papa!'

It was difficult to keep the tears out of one's eyes. One of Joyce's workers had supplied the baby with a bottle and because Caroline couldn't continue to hold it, she propped it around with cushions and set an older child to watch it.

All down the line, responsibilities were handed out and met. A score of helping hands.

The men came in, haggard-faced and unshaven, an endless sea of changing faces. Joyce and her band fed them and kept them up with the news: 'Yes, that's right! Joe Adami walked in a few hours ago!' An incredulous and light-filled: 'Strewth!'

The terrible wind had died away, but the rain was still falling, severely hampering rescue operations. Caroline shuddered when she thought of the power lines that lay everywhere, the danger. Those inside the centre were protected. But outside. . . . She had a feeling of being absolutely remote from herself, searching the scenes of devastation. For Kiall.

Ian was there too. She had to remind herself. The place was swarming again with tired and dirty men. One of them came up to her.

'Caroline?'

'Ian——' She looked at him anxiously. He was paper-white, streaked with mud, utterly exhausted.

'Are you all right?' he demanded.

'More importantly,' she took his arm, 'how are *you*?'

'God, it's awful!' he said hoarsely. 'I didn't realise things could be so bad.'

'Have you seen Kiall?'

His pupils contracted as if he understood the significance of her urgent question. 'He's all right. Cool devil.' He looked down at her hand and gave an irritated laugh. 'Very efficient, very capable. Of course this is his world.'

'I've been so frightened!' Caroline put into words what she had been feeling all day—the frail link man had with life.

Ian laughed on a quick, short breath. 'Don't worry, nothing will happen to him.'

'For you both.' She sensed the frenzy in his mind and sought to lessen it with kindness. 'You look exhausted, Ian. Stay here and I'll get you something to eat.'

Ian sat on the floor with a half a dozen small children crouched beside him. After a while he began to talk to them, tried to make them laugh.

A gentle little Italian lady served Caroline with a plate of sandwiches and a pot of tea. 'For your friend?' she looked at Caroline with understanding. 'I'll find a tray.'

'Many thanks.'

Behind them Joyce's face looked more gaunt and lined than ever. 'There you are, m'dear! I hope that's for yourself?'

'For Ian,' Caroline said calmly. 'He's just come in.'

'That's Ian?' Joyce crinkled up her eyes.

'I think he's had a rough day.'

'I'm sure of it.' Joyce wiped the perspiration from her brow. 'Of course Kiall hasn't come in.'

'Ian's seen him,' Caroline told her.

'Thank God!' Joyce betrayed her anxiety. 'I've been haunted by all the things that could go wrong.'

Ian sipped his tea with something approaching bliss. 'Wonderful . . . thank you.'

She too sat down on the floor and pulled a yellow-clad toddler on to her lap. The little boy sat perfectly still staring at her with huge dark eyes.

'Do you like kids?' Ian sounded surprised.

'Sure I do.' Caroline's fingers stroked the baby's neck and under his plump chin. 'You're beautiful.'

Ian tossed a sandwich into his mouth. 'When do you suppose Stirling is pulling out?'

'He'll let us know.'

'God!' There was an edge of anger in Ian's voice. 'To think this is my vacation!'

'Doesn't it make you feel better to be able to help people?' Caroline asked.

'I've never been one to stick my neck out,' Ian said wryly.

The baby, strangely content, snuggled against Caroline's breast. It gave her such a feeling of tenderness and pleasure, a lovely radiance shone from her face. What joy in having a child of one's own! She let her imagination centre on another little boy: silky black hair and instead of liquid, Mediterranean eyes, a shimmering silver-grey. She would be a good mother, the happiness and wellbeing of her child uppermost. Her own childhood had had to be endured. Any child of hers would never know such cruelty.

'Here we go again!' Ian muttered suddenly.

She looked up quickly as Ian staggered to his feet. 'What is it?'

'Stirling,' he said bluntly.

For the life of her, Caroline couldn't keep the relief out of her eyes. She looked across the room in time to see Kiall walk in. She saw his hand go out and grip an elderly man's shoulder, and saw the old man smile.

'If the people up here had their way,' Ian said sourly, 'he'd be Prime Minister.'

Caroline, sensing his jealousy, kept a guard upon her tongue. The baby was getting sleepy; very heavy against her arm.

Kiall's silver eyes narrowed as he focused on them, then he came across the room.

'He doesn't even look tired,' Ian muttered with primitive antagonism.

He's stronger than we are, Caroline thought. He was coming towards them with deft, purposeful movements, a big man, tough and unsmiling.

'Good work, Randall,' he said, when he reached them.

Ian flushed with pleasure, his enmity forgotten all at once. 'Glad to be of help.'

'All we want now is for the rain to stop.' Kiall leant over and took the baby out of Caroline's arms.

Removed from the comfort of her arms, it could have cried, but it didn't, and one of the Adami sisters came to his side with a smile.

'I'll take the baby, Mr Stirling.'

He nodded his head. 'Thanks, Pina.'

'Did you know Papa was all right?'

'Sure.' He turned his dark head and smiled at the girl; absolutely charming. 'I heard him singing not an hour ago. I thought it was *Rigoletto*.'

'Didn't you know?' Pina was looking up at him with hero-worship.

'There was a hell of a lot of noise at the time.'

Pina laughed and went away and Kiall leaned over Caroline, who was still curled up quietly on the floor. 'I'll take you home before long,' he said.

'I'm all right.' She found, once on her feet, she had to hold on to him for a few moments.

'I don't like your pallor,' he told her. 'You're very pale.'

'It's the heat.'

'She's been coping magnificiently,' Ian was staring at them both as if mesmerised.

Kiall gave a faint shrug of his powerful shoulders. 'I think we can find someone to replace you.'

'I can't go.' Caroline straightened her back in the stifling heat. 'The children have got used to me. It would unsettle them.'

'Have you had anything to eat?' he asked.

'No.' She drew a shaky little breath.

'Right. Let's go.'

They didn't leave the Centre until after midnight, and only then did Caroline find out they had been billeted with the town's senior doctor.

'Kiall ... Kiall!' Doctor Kemp worked his way through the maze of sleeping or crouching bodies. 'Here's the key.'

'Thanks, Viv.' Kiall flicked it in his pocket. 'What time will we see you?'

'Don't worry about me.' The doctor's uplifted hands gestured a little helplessly. 'I think it calms everyone to know I'm here.'

Caroline was unaware she was swaying on her feet and the doctor asked her if she was all right.

'Yes, of course.' She smiled at him with shadowed eyes.

'Sleep, that's the important thing.' Joyce tried to smile and failed, and Kiall got a grip on both women's shoulders.

'Come on, girls. Bed!'

Because she hadn't seen Ian, Caroline concluded correctly that he had been billeted with someone else. She knew damn well she should ask, but she was too tired.

The doctor's house occupied high ground, and as Caroline started to walk up the steps she tripped over some fallen object and a shaft of pain shot through her ankle.

'O . . . *oh!*' It was a pathetic little moan.

'M'dear gel.' Joyce said from the darkness, 'I'm here.'

'What the hell is it now?' Kiall's strong hands reached out to grasp her around the waist.

'My ankle.' Exhaustion made her voice break a little.

'Darling gel,' Joyce asked sharply, 'what's the matter?'

Kiall exhaled slowly. 'Turn on the porch light, Joyce while I see.'

'For heaven's sake, where is it?' Joyce clung tightly to the wooden banister, fearing she might slip.

'Where you'd expect, Joyce, beside the door.'

Stumblingly Joyce made it on to the verandah, swearing wildly inside.

'Good girl!' Kiall rewarded her with a smile, sufficient to make her forgive him.

'I'm all right now.' Caroline straightened up, ashamed of her weakness.

'How about that for bravery, Joyce?' Kiall asked.

'For God's sake, 'Joyce groaned, 'be nice!'

'Do you want me to be nice to you, Caroline?' he drawled.

'It's simply not in you.'

He lifted her into his arms without the slightest difficulty, a trifling featherweight to be carried up the stairs.

'A man's stength,' said Joyce with a certain resentment. 'It's splendid.'

'It would be heavenly, Joyce, if you could find the key,' Kiall told her.

'In your breast pocket, I think.'

'Help yourself.'

They were inside the house, and Joyce went ahead, switching on the lights. It was all very pleasant and comfortable, a haven after what they had seen.

'Let's have a look at that ankle.' Kiall lowered his small burden to the chintz-covered sofa, then went down in front of her.

'It's a lot better now,' Caroline told him stoically. 'I think I just ricked it.'

'Another trick to get attention?' He looked up at her, her small foot in his hand. Instead of looking weary and dishevelled, he looked incredibly handsome.

'You're a horrid man, do you know?' she sighed.

'Now that we've got *that* sorted out. . . .' He returned his attention to her ankle. 'There's a little bit of puffiness there. Nothing to worry about.'

'Lord, I'm for bed,' Joyce burst out. 'Where are we supposed to sleep, Kiall, do you know?'

He stood up and moved across the room to Joyce.

'Leave the main bedroom for Viv in case he turns up and take your pick of the rest. There are three bedrooms and a sleep-out. I don't give a damn where I sleep.'

'That's good!' Joyce said briskly. 'Do you suppose I could have a shower?'

Kiall responded by showing her through the house.

Comfortable on the couch, Caroline found she didn't have the slightest desire to move from there. Her heavy eyes moved around the room animated by bookshelves and paintings and a grand piano in the corner. It was a cheerful house, really. Lived-in. It was also very solidly constructed, with a storm cellar.

'Oh, no!' Kiall came back into the room, looking down at her young, relaxed limbs. 'You can't go to sleep there.'

'Why not?'

'Well, I expect because it's too close to the sleep-out.'

'As a matter of fact, I don't sleepwalk,' she told him.

He made a jeering sound, his silver eyes sparkling. 'I'm not taking your word for it. The things that happen around *you*!'

'I wonder where Ian is?' she said, pretending an anxiety she did not feel.

'Just so long as he's not here,' he answered with hard mockery.

'You had him billeted somewhere else,' she said wonderingly.

'You bet I did.' His voice had tautened to amused impatience.

'Wretched man!' Caroline shook her blonde hair out of its confining coil.

'You'll have a hard time shaking him.'

'Why would I want to?' she asked briefly, her luminous eyes shadowed.

'But you don't want him at all, do you? You contrary little wretch.'

'He's in love with me.' There was an element of challenge in her young voice.

'Here's wishing you a wonderful future.'

She was on her feet so quickly she had to clutch at him to save herself from falling. 'I'm serious!' she said feelingly.

'Girls of—eighteen, is it?—are notorious for their lack of seriousness.'

I love you, she thought, raising her green eyes to his.

'What's this?' he taunted her. 'Another spell?'

'Don't be ridiculous.' She sank her teeth in her bottom lip. 'You're a very unpleasant man.'

Joyce came to the living room door, looking very tired but refreshed from a cold shower. 'Bathroom free, m'dear.'

'What shall I sleep in?' Caroline asked,

'*Please*, Caroline.' Kiall's expression was half rueful, half mocking.

'There are plenty of the good doctor's pyjamas in the closet at the end of the corridor,' Joyce told her. 'From the look of it, he's never even used the tops.'

'I'm sure he can spare you one,' Kiall said pleasantly.

Afterwards Caroline seized on the offer. Her dress was a sorry sight and so snug-fitting around the waist it would have been uncomfortable to sleep in. She paused at Joyce's door to say goodnight, but Joyce was unceremoniously snoring.

And why not? Caroline thought with real affection. Joyce had managed splendidly today and on top of that she had spent all that time on her feet. Very gently she closed the door and padded into the smaller room allotted her.

The central mirror in the old wardrobe showed a diminutive blonde in a long dark blue pyjama jacket. Her hair looked intensely fair, her arms and legs very slender. She sighed, turned out the light and got into bed immediately. No use calling a goodnight to Kiall; he would only reply with something scathing.

After such a long and distressing day it was wonderful to savour the cool comfort of the sheets. But what about the others? The people without a home. Until recently Caroline had thought herself hard done by, but Hungerford's crisis had shown her what real suffering was. How wonderful that the Adami girls had found their father. She could still see the tremendous joy on their faces. With their terrible fear gone, the girls had been transformed into miracles of efficiency. They had all worked so well together.

She turned her face into the pillow and tried to relax. She was overtired, that was it. The wind was rattling the windows, making the branches of the great trees scratch the walls. Kiall was still up; she could see a light. How miraculous that this place, this comfortable house had escaped unharmed! In her imagination she was driving into town again, seeing the devastation. The great hurricane had scythed through the northerly outskirts of the town, whereas this side of the township centre was relatively unharmed—a few houses unroofed, dozens of fallen trees. Joe Adami had worn his bloodstains in triumph. He had been one of the lucky ones. A recently married young couple had been killed outright. Twenty-four and twenty-six—no age to die.

In the darkness grief struck her. She was shocked by the tragedy she had seen, unable to put it out of her mind. She had been so protected all her life. Miserable, yes, but protected. No disaster had ever struck the convent.

After a sleepless half hour she got up. The medicine chest in the bathroom was stocked like a chemist's shop. A couple of asprin might ease her headache, allow her to sleep.

The house was in darkness as she padded slowly along the corridor. The windows were rattling in the kitchen and she decided she had better shut them. To tell the truth she was hungry, but she dared not wake the others.

A chair threatened her progress, striking her knee and she caught at it hurriedly, rattled by the scraping sound it made. If Kiall was a light sleeper, he would undoubtedly let her know about it.

She was almost at the kitchen when he suddenly startled her.

'May I ask what you're doing?'

Her shrill little cry was muffled under the hand across her mouth. With his arm around her, he drew her into the kitchen and shut the door. 'Well?'

With the light on her face it was obvious she had been crying.

'I guess I can't sleep,' she shrugged.

'Likewise,' Kiall nodded his dark head, agreeing with her.

'I just can't believe there could be so much devastation,' Caroline sighed.

'That's the way it is up here.' He leaned back against the door, looking at her.

'You were *out* there,' she pointed out, 'It was worse for you.'

'I should have realised you were strung up.' His dark face had no expression, though he was looking at her intently.

'I was going to shut the kitchen windows.' She put a hand to her temple. 'All that rattling and tapping!'

'I'll do it.' He went past her, leaning across the twin basins of the sink and pulling in the heavy, old-fashioned windows.

'Thank you.' Caroline put her hands in the pockets of the pyjama jacket, all of a sudden intensely conscious of her body beneath. 'I'm sorry I disturbed you.'

'You wanted to.' He turned to face her squarely.

'No.' She shook her head a little helplessly. 'All I wanted was a couple of aspirin.'

'That was why you were so quiet.'

'Knocking into the chair was an accident!'

'That's okay.' Kiall gave her a mocking smile. 'I wasn't asleep.'

'Joyce is,' she said.

'I'm not sure what that means?' His eyes swept over her with a mixture of mockery and derision.

'Then you must be awfully dense!' She was tempted to hit him, but common sense prevailed.

'I shouldn't if I were you.' His expression made it clear he had read her mind. 'What were you crying about anyway?'

'Homes . . . lives that are ripped apart.'

'You're a very sensitive girl.'

'Oh, shut up!' She hated his pitiless mockery. The tears rushed to her eyes again and she dashed them away angrily. 'Good night.'

'What about the aspirin, silly?'

She let go of the door handle and spun around to face him, only he wasn't by the sink any more, but right behind her.

It was a sickness, desire—incurable. The body was more vulnerable than the mind. It betrayed.

'That's what I mean, Caroline,' he said.

'I'll get over it.'

'Why can't you leave it alone?'

She looked at the shape of his mouth, his cleft chin. 'I don't know how,' she said shakily.

He reached for her and she went willingly; a silent, violent confession of a mutual need. There were no whispered endearments, no words at all, but a compulsive, consuming want.

She had never dreamed anything could be so beautiful or so savage, the faint cruelty that increased her profound yielding. Her arousal was such, she was desperate for more. Not here, not crushed against his body, but freedom to lie beside him all night long, his skin on hers, his head against her heart. It was unbearable to feel this way.

The drumming in her ears was so loud and heavy she scarcely heard what he said, so finally he shook her so her hair cascaded over her shoulder.

'I won't let this happen.' There was a kind of anguish on his dark face though his voice lashed her.

'Kiall?' she murmured dazedly.

'How do you want this to end?'

'Just the two of us together.'

'No matter who you are . . . what you are?'

'Who am I?' she asked. 'Tell me. In your arms I forget everything.'

'Well, I can't.' The arms that held her away from him were as implacable as his voice. 'All right, I want you. Right now I could take you in a way neither of us would ever forget but I'm not such a monster.'

Caroline bent her head into her hands. 'Oh, *stop* it! I love you, Kiall.'

'You can't mean that.'

'I do.' The shadows beneath her green eyes were violet, but when she straightened her head and looked at him, her glance was unwavering. 'Inevitable, I suppose. Heredity, something like that.'

'Do you realise you could be Martin's child?' he demanded.

'So we're cousins. Our mothers weren't related in any way.' His hands were clenched so hard on her upper arms she gave a little involuntary whimper. 'Please, Kiall, you're hurting me!'

'I've never wanted more to hurt you. What the hell's the matter with me?'

She gave a low, tremulous laugh. 'You loathe yourself for being vulnerable. For being, even for a moment, in a woman's power. What happened to Martin has stayed with you, made you retreat from tenderness and love. I think you're afraid of me, afraid of any woman who can make you lose your precious control.'

'But you haven't, have you?' A cold hauteur edged his tone.

'No.' At that moment she despised herself. 'I haven't the experience to really make you lose your head.'

'Do you think not?' he asked in a harsh, clipped voice. 'Everything about you drives me to excess.' He took her head in his hands, imprisoning it, and sought her mouth.

The initiative was so entirely his, her eyes closed and her head fell back against his shoulder. She was as helpless as a child, her mouth moving frantically under his, her whole body trembling. If he settled this thing now, she had nobody to blame but herself.

Oh God! she cried aloud in her head. Was this the way lives were destroyed? Passion that towered only to cast one up on the rocks.

Heat clung to the small bedroom where he carried her, but instead of swooping over her he flung her, almost at once, on to the bed.

'Try not to goad me,' he muttered. 'It's not very clever.'

Caroline couldn't answer even if she wanted to—but then it didn't matter, for he had gone.

CHAPTER TEN

Two days before Christmas, a special messenger delivered a package to Joyce's door.

'For you, m'dear.'

'Oh?' Caroline looked up from a Chinese jigsaw puzzle in mild abstraction.

'Jewellery, I'd say.' Joyce sat down at a Regency card table.

'Why?' Caroline began to open the small package.

'The feel of it, m'dear. I used to get packages like that as a gel.'

'It must be from Ian,' Caroline said rather flatly.

Joyce didn't answer; a little tired of Ian herself.

Inside was an olive green velvet case, and inside that a long lustrous rope of pearls.

'Bless my soul!' Joyce inhaled so deeply, she almost gagged.

'Damn them all!' muttered Caroline.

"Who, m'dear?' Joyce reacted to that strangely bitter voice.

'Surely you've seen these pearls before?' Caroline took them out of the case and let them hang from her hand.

Joyce's noble brow knotted ferociously. 'They're not . . .?'

'They *are*. There's even a message.' She picked up a small card and turned it over. 'I thought you might not have forgotten our conversation.'

'Forgotten?' Joyce looked at her a little helplessly.

'I told you Miss Stirling paid me a visit. What I

didn't tell you was, she promised me these pearls if I'd go away.'

Joyce was so incensed she cried out in a loud voice, startling Molly who heaved herself up and barked. 'How *could* she?' Molly barked again in that deep, powerful reproachful voice. Who was there?

'She'd dare anything!' Caroline waved the labrador to her side and patted her. 'No price too dear to get rid of me.'

'Those pearls would be worth a small fortune!' Joyce gritted through her teeth. 'How dare she insult you!'

'Why don't I just take them and go?' Caroline sighed.

'Because, m'dear,' Joyce said kindly, 'that's not your style.'

'Miss Stirling doesn't appear to have any difficulty underrating me.'

'To be absolutely frank,' Joyce confided, 'Thea underrates us all. She's the most appalling snob, and in the end, money, position—it doesn't mean anything. I could have put myself in prison, but look at me!'

'Not everyone is like you, Joyce,' Caroline murmured. 'What am I going to do about these?'

'Take them back,' Joyce told her without hesitation. 'Accuse her to her face.'

'Aren't they flying off to England tomorrow?'

'So you'll have to hurry.' Joyce flung up her hands. 'Compared to Thea you may be poor, m'dear, but think yourself rich!'

Caroline laughed. 'I may upset her.'

'Be cool,' Joyce advised. 'No need to throw them in her face.'

Hilda greeted Caroline at the front door, looking faintly puzzled. 'Why, how are you, miss?'

'Fine thank you, Hilda,' Caroline smiled. 'Would Miss Stirling be in?'

'Are you expected, miss?' Hilda paused, clearly not wanting to disturb Miss Stirling.

'Actually, no.'

'Then you don't know Miss Stirling and Mr Kiall are leaving for England tomorrow? They go home every Christmas to visit Mr Kiall's mother.'

'Yes, I did know,' Caroline said pleasantly. 'Nevertheless, my business is fairly pressing.'

Hilda smiled again, uncertainly. 'If you'd just take a seat, miss, I'll tell Miss Stirling you're here.'

'Thank you.' For the second time Caroline found herself within the distinguished residence, surveying the marble floor.

A few moments later Hilda came back, her look indicating that all was well. 'Would you come this way, please, miss.'

Miss Stirling was in her sitting room, ensconced behind an exquisite ormolu-mounted bureau.

'Thank you, Hilda,' she said dismissively.

Hilda gave Caroline an almost conpiratorial gaze.

'Surely you're not here to thank me?' Thea Stirling said with a certain surprise, when Hilda had gone.

'Thank you for a bit of bluster?' Caroline smiled and unzipped her handbag. 'No, Miss Stirling, I'm here to return the family pearls.'

Thea Stirling stared at her, astonished. 'You can't imagine you'll get a better offer?'

'Considering what they're worth, no.' Caroline extracted the velvet case from her bag, gazed at it a moment as if fascinated, then set it down on the tulipwood desk. 'Kiall wouldn't really thank you for interfering, you know.'

'Believe me, my dear, I would never tell him. If

that's what's worrying you.' Thea Stirling gazed at her visitor with ruthless contempt.

'Then how would you account for the loss of your pearls?'

'Don't be a fool!' Thea Stirling sat up stiffer in her gilt wood chair. 'I have other pearls.'

'Like that?'

Thea shrugged. 'Kiall expects me to be well groomed, but he doesn't pay a great deal of attention to what I wear.'

'What about your sister-in-law?' Caroline persisted. 'Women notice these things far more than men.'

Thea smiled at her sardonically. 'I can merely say I left them at home. Let's be reasonable, my dear. My offer holds, a silent agreement between us. Take the pearls and go as far away as you like.'

'And you're not sure if I'm your niece or not?' Caroline looked at her levelly.

'You're wicked, like your mother,' Thea said harshly. 'An unscrupulous, conniving little upstart!'

Caroline zipped up her handbag and walked calmly to the door. 'And you're paranoid on the subject. I'm really very harmless, Miss Stirling—as my poor little mother was. Leave her in peace.'

'Then you're rejecting my offer?' Thea Stirling stood up, her handsome face rather ghastly with hate.

'I never considered it in the first place.' On the threshold Caroline paused, the light turning her silver-gilt hair into a shining aureole around her small, fine-boned face.

'Be careful, my dear,' Thea warned.

Caroline shrugged that off. 'I'm here now, Miss Stirling, and I'm staying, whether you're my enemy or not!'

Thea Stirling went the most peculiar shade and her

iron fingers closed around a heavy cut-glass paper-weight. 'Can't you have a little pity for me? For Kiall?' she cried.

'I love him.' In a kind of terror Caroline heard her own voice, the passion that was in it.

'You ... *creature!*' Thea shrieked. She lifted the hand with the paperweight in it and threw it with all the force that was in her.

But Caroline escaped. She moved just in time, slamming into the taut body of the man who held her.

'What in God's name is going on?' Kiall held Caroline so tightly she ached.

'Kiall ... *Kiall!*' Thea Stirling collapsed in her chair, crying bitterly.

'What are you doing here, Caroline?' Kiall's eyes were blazing and he looked as if he might shake her.

'Ask your aunt.' Her delicate face was pale, her eyes enormous in the light of what she thought of as Thea Stirling's insane anguish.

'I'm asking you.' He turned her around and held her shoulders.

'Do you Stirlings care for anyone else but your-selves?' demanded Caroline shakily.

'Please tell me!' he insisted.

She gave a little fluttering sigh and looked away. 'I told you before, your aunt hates me, and you wouldn't listen. She hated my mother and she hates me. She believes she loves you the same way she loved her brother. But she doesn't. She doesn't know what love is. Just hatred and revenge. She does things behind your back, just as she betrayed her own brother.'

'Don't listen to her, Kiall!' Thea Stirling shook with the force of her violent emotions.

'He'd better listen,' Caroline said. 'You plotted to destroy your brother's life. You thought my mother wasn't good enough for him, so you lied and lied. Edward Marshall helped you, the willing pawn. They did love each other, Martin and Deborah, and because of it they paid the ultimate price.'

'Shut her up, for God's sake!' Thea cried.

'What if you'd hit her, Thea?' Kiall asked in a strange voice.

'I'd have been glad!' The words ripped out of her, the hatred and the venom.

There was something so terrible about it, both Kiall and Caroline turned away.

'You see?' Caroline laughed a little brokenly. 'No one is going to welcome me into the bosom of the family.'

He drew a harsh and tearing breath. 'She'll never, ever, attempt to injure you again.'

'Then you'd better watch her constantly.' Caroline's young face was quietly tortured. 'I suppose when my mother was killed she was happy.'

'Don't say that!' Kiall spun her towards him almost lifting her off the ground. 'You can't know how she's suffered all these years.'

'Yes, I'm sure of that.' Caroline looked full into his glittering eyes. 'Just as I'm sure she deserved to.'

'*Caroline!*'

She swallowed painfully. 'Both of you have done all you could to make me go.'

'There's too much behind us,' he said.

Something made Caroline pull back her shoulders and tilt her head. 'So long, cousin,' she said sadly. 'Enjoy your trip away.'

When she told Ian she was going back with him, he couldn't believe it.

'But, sweetheart, how marvellous! I knew you'd come to your senses.'

Come to her senses. Come to the end of hope. No matter what Kiall felt for her neither of them could wipe away the past. There would always be a mystery, a pattern of love–hate that could be repeated. If she stayed what they both wanted and feared was bound to happen—a physical passion that would pull her under. Kiall would survive, hardened by his stormy background.

Joyce was understandably upset, and Paddy when he heard she was leaving used the mournful news as an excuse to get drunk. He even turned up at three o'clock in the morning trying to stop her and got a good dressing down from Joyce.

It was Joyce who insisted she should stay at least until after the New Year.

'Why not, m'dear?' They were rather gloomily decorating a splendid twelve-foot-high tree. 'There's no Thea to tackle. She'll be away at least until the end of January.'

'No Kiall.' Wretchedly Caroline hung a glittering bauble.

'I expect you'd have to fall in love with him!' Joyce choked back a sigh. 'I could fall in love with him myself, I think. Albeit a little late in life.'

Caroline had the good sense not to enquire Joyce's age. In any case, she was sure Joyce would straightforwardly tell a lie.

The news of Caroline's plans for departure had someone else's wholehearted approval.

Coming out of the town's main real estate office Caroline encountered Danae Edgeley, dressed up to the nines and in a torrent of conversation with a person she professed she detested.

'Hello there!' Caroline called with a glint of cynicism in her eyes.

For an instant Colin Rayment looked vague, but Danae very nearly pounced.

'Why, Miss Marshall!'

It was as good a way as any to address her, Caroline thought. Of late she had got into the habit of thinking of herself as a nobody.

'Lovely day!' It was true the sun was shining brilliantly.

'I say, don't go.' Danae stared after her. 'I thought we might have a cup of coffee.'

Colin Rayment raised his brows. 'I didn't know you two girls were pally,' he commented.

'We are now!' Danae laughed gaily. She put out her hand and touched Colin's sleeve. 'I'll leave it to you. Come, if you can.'

'In any case,' he said dryly, 'Kiall's not here.'

Caroline took a deep breath as Danae caught up to her. 'I didn't realise you and Mr Rayment were friendly.'

Danae glanced at her with a certain malicious pride. 'Poor Colin! He's in love with me. It seems the cat can look at the Queen.'

Caroline coughed.

'And fancy, you're leaving us!' Danae's glowing face betrayed her relief. 'Your idea or Kiall's?'

'It seemed tactless to stay.'

Danae gave her a bright, blue-eyed glance. 'Young girls always fall for someone terribly unsuitable. It's like getting measles—unavoidable, you might say.'

'I might, if I knew what you were talking about,' Caroline countered.

'Don't be embarrrassed,' Danae smiled at her kindly, 'I know exactly what it feels like. I fell in love with Kiall when I was a mere child.'

'God knows that was a while ago,' Caroline commented, cool as a cucumber. 'Look, I don't think this is a good idea, a cup of coffee. You don't like me and I've decided about you.'

'Not very polite, are you, dear?' Danae said acidly. 'But then it's not easy to be nice when your nose is out of joint. I believe Thea put you in your place well and truly.'

They had come to a near halt outside an alfresco coffee shop and Danae paused and put her parcels down. 'It isn't very important now, in any case—Thea's jealousy or mine. You're going.'

Caroline's beautiful, luminous eyes were unsmiling. 'It's going to be difficult for you all the same,' she shrugged.

Danae's little laugh came out the wrong way. 'Whatever do you mean?'

'I wouldn't care to have Miss Stirling for an in-law or whatever.'

'Sit down,' Danae said abruptly. 'Go on, sit down. I won't eat you.'

'Actually I'm not a nervous person.' Caroline just stood there staring at the gaily coloured tablecloths.

'You want me to make a scene?'

Caroline hesitated, then sat down. 'No,' she said dryly. 'That'd be a crashing bore!'

'You know, you interest me,' said Danae, taking off her sunglasses. 'Under other circumstances, I might even like you.'

'What's preventing you now?' Caroline picked up the menu, simply for something to do.

'My goodness,' Danae enclaimed, her blue eyes wide, 'I simply couldn't let you have Kiall. I think I'd shoot you first.'

'Really?' Caroline shrugged.

'I'd do something,' said Danae with some exasperation. 'Cool little piece, aren't you? I can see why Thea had so much trouble.'

'She did rather speed things up,' Caroline admitted.

'Of course I'll get rid of her when the time comes,' Danae muttered.

'Of course!' Caroline said sweetly. 'The same pistol?'

'Don't worry,' Danae said curtly. 'I'll be mistress in my own home.'

'Maralaya?' Caroline's lovely mouth twisted.

'Don't think I've waited all these years for nothing!' Danae seemed impelled to talk. 'I've never known any man crueller to me than Kiall, but I want him.' She gave a brittle little laugh. 'He's the reason I'm twenty-eight and not married.'

'We all have our troubles.'

A very handsome Italian waiter paused by their table, caught up in the vision of two very attractive young women framed by an umbrella of different colours.

'May I bring you something?' he murmured, looking admiringly from one to the other. The little blonde was his choice.

'Two coffees,' Danae said briskly, in a no-nonsense voice. 'Black.'

'A cappuccino for me,' Caroline smiled to balance the commanding tone.

'*Si!*' The waiter brushed a non-existent crumb off the table. Such sweetness in a smile!

'You realise you shouldn't have come up here in the first place?' Danae leaned forward with apparent concern. 'I mean, it was terrible what happened to Martin Stirling and your mother—like a movie. In all fairness to Thea, it's easy to understand why she hates you.'

'Why should she?' Caroline said calmly. 'What have I done to her?'

'Daddy spotted you one day in town,' Danae offered by way of explanation. 'It gave him quite a shock. The thing is, you're the image of your mother—according to Thea, an empty-headed little adventuress.'

The frightful inaptness of the word made Caroline shudder. 'Do you really think a man like Martin Stirling would fall in love with a mindless little fool?'

'No,' Danae answered bluntly. 'She must have been very beautiful, very refined. Daddy said as much and he has excellent taste. He also said she was no match for Thea Stirling.'

'Thea Stirling didn't go unscathed,' Caroline pointed out, 'she carries her scars. It's terrible to realise what jealousy will do—set in motion a chain of events that can lead to tragedy.'

'I'm sure you're right!' Danae frowned. 'In many ways Thea is a sinister sort of woman. But you don't know Kiall's mother and sisters. They're beautiful! And very dear to me. Why, only the other day I had a letter from Nina. She said in it that all of them have one dream—to see Kiall married. To *me*!'

'I suppose they don't understand why you've both taken such a time,' Caroline commented demurely.

Danae obviously didn't feel like joking. 'Kiall's fault!' She lifted back a glossy tendril of her short dark hair. 'He's resisted marriage for a long time. I've always thought it was something to do with the old tragedy. He adored his uncle. Then when his father was killed and his mother nearly had a breakdown he decided he didn't really want to care deeply about anyone. He's the sort of man that might feel trapped.'

'I agree with you.'

'Exactly.' Danae wasn't looking at her. 'When you

turned up it really scared me. Not your fault, really, I suppose. It was odd, though, Kiall's reaction. I know him very well. Somehow you got to him.' She raised her blue eyes and stared admonishingly into Caroline's face. 'It's the damned resemblance—the old story. It surely must have occurred to you that there are some tortuous hiding places in Kiall. He's a very complex man.'

'It's always best to know what you're up against!' Caroline looked ahead to indicate that the waiter was coming.

'There we are, *signorina*,' he slipped the cup of coffee from the tray to beside Caroline's hand.

'Thank you. That will do nicely,' said Danae.

Outrageous, such brusqueness in a woman!

Danae sipped at her coffee and emitted a little cry. 'Goodness, that's *hot*!' She put the coffee cup down again and slumped back in her chair. 'I imagine he might have come around a bit quicker if I hadn't given him what he wanted.'

'And what was that?' Caroline decided she was absolutely impervious to pain.

'You're not a child,' Danae said in a low, intense voice. 'Kiall has been my lover for years. There's never been anyone else for either of us. And yet he wouldn't marry me. Until now.' Cautiously and very slowly she withdrew a thin golden chain from inside the neckline of her beautifully simple blue dress. 'This is what he gave me before he left.'

It was unmistakably an engagement ring; an exceptionally fine emerald-cut diamond ring.

For an instant Caroline thought a dead faint would overtake her. The blood seemed to drain away from her heart.

'*Caroline?*' The tone of Danae's voice braced her.

'Are you all right?'

I'll never be all right again.

Danae gave an uncomfortable laugh. 'I hadn't thought it would affect you so badly!'

Caroline didn't answer for a moment, because she couldn't.

'I mean, you barely know him. Please don't be offended when I say you'll get over it. Kiall is a fascinating man, but he is, without question, difficult. He's the kind of man that knows how to make a woman suffer.'

Caroline formed her words with difficulty. 'You've no idea how I envy you. But my curiosity is aroused. How come you're wearing such an expensive ring there?'

'It means such a lot to me,' Danae clutched the ring to her breast. 'But of course, it's not official yet. Kiall has to tell his mother first. We're hoping she'll come back with him. She so loved Maralaya in the old days.'

She's waiting, I suppose, for me to say something, Caroline thought. She thinks she owns him and now she's claiming her due; marriage. It will sink in later, much later, when I'm alone.

'What are you thinking about with those big, sad eyes?' Danae asked.

'It doesn't matter at all,' Caroline shrugged.

'I don't want to hurt you,' said Danae, looking for a moment truly anxious. 'It's hell, first love.'

I won't forget.

'Why, I bet you'll be in love a dozen times before the year is out.' Danae rattled on, restless in the face of the younger girl's tightly controlled distress.

With a tremendous effort Caroline stood up, her coffee untouched. She put a few coins down on the table and smiled at Danae's rather unhappy expression.

'I won't see you again, but every happiness for the future.'

'Don't be ridiculous,' said Danae. 'I want you to come to my New Year party. Bring your friend.'

'Actually Joyce is having a few people over.'

'But that would be ghastly! Joyce's friends—they must be *sixty*!'

'I've always found I like older people.' Caroline told the truth. 'Goodbye, Danae. I hope life is good to you.'

By some feat of pride she was able to move through the tables gracefully, even nod to the young waiter, who smiled at her.

She was an old hand at pain—but nothing like this! The dazzling light struck at her, the heat of the sun pouring down. She had to act as if nothing had happened, keep on walking, make it to the car. Someone blasted her as she attempted to cross the street, said something to her that was lost in the racket of the traffic.

'Strewth, love!' A wiry hand clutched her on the shoulder. 'Are ya trying to kill yaself on purpose or by chance?'

'Paddy!' Caroline blinked her green eyes.

'Gawd, love!' Paddy put his left hand on his bald head. 'Ya look bloody awful!'

'I do feel a little faint,' she confessed.

Paddy reacted in the only way he knew how. 'What ya need,' he said with certainty, 'is a stiff drink.'

Joyce knew her young friend was distraught, but she could do nothing. It had to end, the thing between Kiall and Caroline, but did Danae have to blab about their coming engagement. So cruel!

The days spun away in a ghastly trace when it

seemed to Caroline that nothing had any concrete meaning. Ian, who was overstaying his welcome without realising it, was doing everything in his power to 'understand' her, being a real friend, but while Caroline often appeared to be sitting there listening to him, she never heard a word. Nothing could erase the truth, too unbearable to contemplate. She had known from the beginning that Kiall was dangerous; that he had a certain tendency towards cruelty. She had been a willing victim, and in the end she felt as if she was dying.

There was little or no wait on the sale of the farm. Tom McKay, the real estate agent, told her with a shake of his big head: 'Absolutely top dollar, Miss Marshall. A broken-down old place too.'

Maybe it was, but it still attracted her. The earliest chapter of her life had been spent there, though she remembered nothing of the heat and the prolifically flowering wilderness.

'I'll have to go over, Joyce, and collect a few things,' she said.

Joyce, who was repotting plants in the bush house, pushed back her hair. 'I can't allow you to go alone.'

'Don't worry, I won't stumble over another snake,' Caroline assured her.

'If you'll wait a while I'll come with you.' Joyce twined a Hoya around a light support.

'No, let me say goodbye to it alone.'

'Life—what a jungle!' Joyce groaned. She had grown very fond of Caroline and the girl's unhappiness was almost as bad for her. 'I know, I'll send Paddy over. He can help you shift out your books.'

Caroline nodded and patted Joyce's arm.

The air around the farmhouse was like quicksilver, a colour to confound memory. Would she ever forget the colour of Kiall's eyes? If he had been plain, or even like Ian, it wouldn't seem so romantic. Dark, handsome men were the devil, but finally when she thought of him, it was always his eyes. So much life in them. Not love. Danae was going to be miserable if she wanted that. The extraordinary part was, she didn't feel jealous, not as if another woman had replaced her. No one had replaced her. Kiall had admitted she was in his bloodstream, but he was going to forget her. A man who could do just that. Wonderful to be a man!

When she let herself inside the house she saw the broken glass in the side windows had been replaced. Kiall must have done that. With her hand outstretched, she stood near the shutters, recalling how it had been on that terrible day. From the shelter and protection of the convent into a furious, ill-advised passion. She had grown up too fast; branded by a tall, wide-shouldered man.

It was very hot and still inside the house and she set about selecting those books from the bookcase she wanted to take. Some proof that she indeed had a family. There was Edward Marshall's handwriting over very many of them. Who was he? Her father? Certainly her mother's husband. She really couldn't bear to think about it any more and the Stirlings were determined at all costs to keep her out. Rich, arrogant, ruthless. She wished to God she could shrug their memory away.

Half way through her packing she went to the kitchen to make some coffee, then she carried it back into the living room. The bungalow seemed full of ghosts. She wasn't sure if she didn't believe in them. There was the oddest feeling that she was being guided by a stronger hand.

The leather-bound books, the classics, she had decided to take. There were several resting on the very top shelves. T's. Tolkien, Tolstoy . . . *The Lord of the Rings, War and Peace, Anna Karenina*. She went back into the kitchen for a chair. Whatever she thought of Edward Marshall, like her, he must have been a great reader.

She lifted two of the dusty volumes down, and as she did so she dislodged a small leather-bound book that had been slotted between the larger books and pushed to the back of them. Over the years, the covers had stuck together, but now the smaller book fell, sapphire blue in colour, stamped with gold lettering: *Diary*.

Without being aware of it, Caroline gave a little cry of anguish. She jumped off the chair, staring at the book for a moment before she picked it up. Inside was some revelation. She just *knew* it. She brushed her hands before her eyes, certain she was holding her mother's possession—a feeling that came through strongly though as yet she hadn't even opened the cover.

Tears misted her eyes, echoes of all the terrible loneliness she had endured. She carried the diary to the old sofa and sat down, her hands not quite steady.

The flyleaf bore a name: Deborah Marshall.

A small neat hand, no discernible trait of character. The one person who knew the truth. A vein in her temple began to pulse. Almost with trepidation Caroline turned the page, all sense of the present receding as she returned to the past.

The first entry was dated, as were the others, and she gasped softly as she realised these entries had been made almost a year before her mother had been killed. She read:

Teddy has started to torment me again about Martin.

CHAPTER ELEVEN

THE two weeks in Melbourne passed in a blur of comings and goings; of Ian's mother sitting opposite her, blue eyes boring into her as she tried to decide whether Caroline, in fact, would make a good wife for her beloved only son. In the end she must have decided the answer was yes, for Caroline had extreme difficulty getting out of the house.

'Could you tell me *why* you want to go away?' In his own surroundings Ian's manner had reverted to faintly hectoring.

'Something about the heat,' Caroline explained. 'I don't know.'

'But Brisbane's not the big city Melbourne is!' Ian shook his fair head as though she was going out of her mind.

'I like it. Something about the light and the air and all those glorious beaches.'

'But you don't know anybody!' Ian made one of the many plaintive sounds he had been making lately.

'I don't know anybody here,' Caroline shrugged a little wretchedly. The Randalls had been very kind to her in their fashion.

'Of course, the real reason,' Ian said vindictively, 'is that you lost your head over Stirling. Very imprudently too, I might mention. For one thing, I doubt if he's got it in him to care for any woman. Somehow that's the way with these damned irresistible types.'

'I'm sorry, Ian.' Caroline could see his abject misery.

'You'll be sorrier still if you don't marry me. Mother and I have talked about it when you weren't here and we've decided you'll make me an eminently suitable wife when you're a little older. Mother has been assessing you pretty thoroughly, you know. You're lovely to look at, reasonably intelligent, and you'll be able to hold your own in the sort of world we inhabit. Altogether, you're an asset.'

'That's very gracious of you, Ian,' Caroline smiled remotely. 'Your opinion means a lot to me.'

'Well, naturally, you're a little young and you're sometimes . . . .' Ian reached for a drink to fortify himself. 'That business with Stirling really had me worried. He lives in a different world, Caroline, a different world from yours and mine. I won't give you a lecture, but you simply mustn't think of him any more. I heard he was getting married to his long-time girlfriend, anyway.'

'Every now and again men do what they're supposed to do,' Caroline said with a touch of tartness. 'You've been very kind to me, Ian, and I appreciate it, but you haven't been listening too closely to what I've been saying. I'm not reasonably intelligent. I'm very bright. My T.E. score will get me into any university I care to go to. I'm not a deserted waif, I'm a young woman with, I hope, a little spirit and a sense of independence. Because I haven't got plenty of money, I'm going to enrol in a teacher training college and get my degree at night. I've been speaking to my old teacher at the convent and she agrees I'll make an excellent teacher. I'm going to try, anyway. I know now what real tragedy is and I've got plenty going for me. One way and another, Ian, I'm going to make out. On my *own*.'

Many times in the next few months Caroline was to

remember that pronouncement, and when heartbreak seized her she went out with any one of her new-found friends, or they all went out in a group together. She had learnt that one had to reach out to people, and much of the old reserve, the holding back, had gone. All of her friends, all in her own age group, all slogging students, wrested every opportunity to enjoy themselves in their free time. Although she was only small and slight, she was a natural athlete, so there was plenty of swimming and surfing and tennis. One of the boys, discovering she had a natural swing and a good eye, had started to take her golfing and, of course, all the physical activity prevented her from brooding.

Yet it only took an aroma: the scent of gardenias, or boronia, the dry, pungent air, and it all crashed over her, in spite of herself. Would there ever be any release from the past? The boys she knew said very nice things to her. Some had even kissed her, and the awkwardness had been sweet, but there was no drowning, blinding joy. Afterwards she could always draw back and tease them a little so they went away laughing, but when Kiall had touched her, his possession had been absolute.

At those times she would whisper to herself the admission: 'I love you and I suppose I always will.'

The next day she would get up and go to school and lose herself in classes and the usual student activities and movements. She was even voted on to the student council when it became apparent she was no frivolous blonde but a serious academic who knew how to exert herself. In short, she got through her days successfully, but at night, with her studies over, she succumbed. If only she were as innocent now as she was then! Only a short time ago she didn't know about love; about men and women. Knowing Kiall had changed her life. From now on she would always want the impossible.

On Easter Saturday she stood in the cool of her room and slipped on a new dress. It was green, the same colour as her eyes, and more expensive than anything she had ever bought. Tonight it was her friend Nan Baker's birthday party, and the Bakers did things in real style. No casual gear tonight, but real dressing, and the girls had been thrilled. A great part of the charm of being a woman was dressing like one.

Caroline clipped some pretty earrings on her ears and stood back from the mirror to spray herself with fragrance. She looked altogether more daring than she usually looked. The beaded camisole top of her dress was fairly low cut, definitely body-shaping, and she wore more make-up than usual, with the result that she looked older and even to her own eyes unexpectedly alluring. It had to be a touch of mascara that made her eyes so big and green; a deeper-toned lipstick that drew attention to the warm curves of her mouth. She would have had to be blind not to know she looked good.

Her escort for the evening, David, arrived right on time, telling her she looked 'fantastic' and clinging to her side all night long. It was a beautiful party with the girls like flowers in their prettiest dresses, the boys almost unrecognisable out of their jeans and properly groomed. That night Caroline tried not to think of anything but enjoying herself. At eighteen years of age life had plenty of good things to offer. She would become a High School teacher—the best. One day she might even be headmistress. She wanted lots of things . . . what? She wanted children. She loved children. With them she could release all her latent tenderness. Bad luck she had fallen so violently in love with the wrong man, just like that. Even now she gravitated towards the older man. She couldn't take anyone in her own age group at all seriously. So she was having a good time. Pretending she was having a good time.

David walked her to her door, his attractive, thin-featured face almost radiant. 'Say, that was a great party!'

'Every minute of it,' Caroline laughed.

'Going to ask me in?'

'No.' Caroline turned around to answer that lopsided smile.

'A kiss goodnight?' David put out one hand and drew it down the silky, shining length of Caroline's hair. 'Gosh, I love your hair. I just hope you never cut it.'

'If I don't I'll look like a mermaid,' she smiled.

'You can come out and sit in our pool all day.' In the overhead light he could see her clearly. 'Come on, Caro, give us a kiss goodnight. That's not a lot to ask.' He gave her hair a small tug.

'It could be,' she said. Everything sometimes. Molten fire.

'Don't be mean!' he pleaded.

'Goodnight, David.' She turned up her face, but instead of giving her the usual light, sweet salute, David reckoned it was about time he proved he was indisputably a mature man. He trapped Caroline within his young, strong arms, took a deep breath, like a swimmer intending to stay down a long time, and kissed her with a lot of ardency and a decided lack of technique.

It was funny and immensely touching. Caroline felt a hundred years old, or at very least, his mother.

When he released her, she found herself patting him, rather like an exuberant puppy. 'Goodnight, David. Thank you for bringing me home.'

'Thank *you*,' he said breathlessly. 'I'm afraid Dad wants me to help him build a retaining wall in the morning, but I'll give you a ring about lunchtime. We might pick up Nan and Christian and go ten-pin bowling.'

'We'll see,' Caroline responded a little vaguely. There were worse things to do.

She waited outside the door of her unit until he reached his car, and only then did she notice the bigger car that was parked a short distance behind it. The interior lights came on as the occupant got out and for a moment she came quite close to fainting. Who else looked like that? Moved in that lithe, almost pantherish way?

David took off noisily, with a friendly blast of the horn despite the time, and Caroline wished desperately that she could call him back. She wished she could even move.

'*Caroline?*'

He spoke to her from the base of the stairs.

She didn't move, didn't speak, but she couldn't deny the terrible rush of emotion. I have nothing to fear, she thought bravely. The responses of my body are beyond me, but I *do* have control of my mind.

He came up the stairs, more shockingly destructive in reality than he had ever been in her dreams.

'It's taken me months to find you.' His voice was low-pitched, vibrating with some emotion of his own.

'And how did you find me now?' She had to fight what she saw in him, the distinct power.

He answered a little bitterly. 'Joyce finally gave in and told me.'

'And to think I trusted her!'

Kiall glanced down at the key in her hand and took it from her.

'Why don't you ask?' Had he ever asked?

'I guess I'm not the asking type.' He opened the door and waited for her to precede him.

The surprising thing was that she obeyed—an involuntary reflex action. In the face of his personality and the inborn assumption of command one felt impelled to.

'I expected you to be alone.' He swept a shimmering glance around the room.

'I'm a loner.' Caroline spoke coolly, controlling her agitation.

'I thought *I* was too. It's a shock to find out you need one person utterly.'

'And that's yourself?' Caroline put her evening purse down and faced him. 'Joyce wrote me that you never did get around to marrying Danae.'

'I thought one thoroughly miserable person was enough,' he explained.

She shrank back from his words as though each one was a blow. 'What are you doing here, Kiall?'

'That's simple. To see you.'

She turned to face him, her green eyes darkened to deepest jade. 'Whatever for? I . . . do . . . not . . . want . . . to . . . see *you!*'

'No?' Kiall threw back his head in the same old arrogant fashion. 'Do you think I can't see how you're trembling? Do you think I don't know what you're feeling inside?' His brilliant gaze slipped over her face and bare shoulders, the slight, very feminine lines of her body.

'Do we really have to go into this?' Her voice was taut to the point of breaking. 'Surely you're not trying to resurrect the old questions?'

He slumped rather wearily into an armchair. 'Can you offer me a drink?'

Because she couldn't, she almost found herself apologising. 'I'm sorry, I've only coffee. I don't drink at all.'

'And neither do your gentlemen callers?' He stood up, very tall and rather edgy.

'Why don't we go into the kitchen?' she suggested.

'God, what a place to live!' He sounded as if he would be stifled in an attractive two-bedroomed home unit. 'Is this yours?'

'I rent it.' Caroline moved hurriedly ahead of him, desperate not to come within a foot of bodily contact.

'Beehives,' he said indifferently.

'We're not all millionaires!'

His handsome mouth twisted. 'It's always best to aim for the top.'

'Exactly.' Caroline put the kettle on. 'How long have you been waiting?'

'A couple of hours before that incredible good-night.'

'David is one of my suitors,' she said, fairly lightly.

'I'm surprised his family let him out after ten,' Kiall said dryly.

'He's nineteen.'

'I'm not at all surprised.'

She stretched up to take cups and saucers out of the cupboard, angry at the ironic tone of his voice.

'What about Danae?' she asked. 'How did she feel when you let her go?'

'Who?'

'You're a callous beast!'

'Now why in the world are we talking about Danae?'

'You were going to marry her.' She set the cups down rather jarringly in their gold-rimmed saucers.

'It seems a shame to contradict you when you've got

it so firmly in mind,' he retorted.

'Stop watching me!' Caroline was starting to lose her control.

'I've got to, if you don't mind.' He sat down on the edge of the table and unloosened his tie. 'You're the only thing in the whole goddamned place I want to look at.' His face too was showing sign of an unbearable tension. 'Whatever made you decide to stay in Queensland? I was sure you'd gone back to Melbourne and that character Randall sent me on a wild goose chase.'

'I suppose he was trying to protect me.'

'No, darling, he was just plain jealous.'

The endearment, even in a sarcastic voice, turned her heart over. The kettle started to whistle and she turned it off. There was only instant coffee too. Nothing he was used to.

'Only Joyce told me at the right moment when I was ready to call in private detectives,' Kiall added.

Her hand was trembling so much the cup swerved abruptly and a little of the boiling water splashed on her hand. She gave a little muffled cry of pain and he seemed to leap towards her. 'Damn it, damn it, that was my fault!'

He had her hand, holding it under the cold water, and she was lost. There was no end to feeling, only layer upon layer of protective skin. Now it was being stripped away from her, and she knew it with her mind as well as her subjugated body. She loved Kiall. It was that simple. There was no room in her life for anyone else.

'Does it hurt much?' His voice was low and curiously caressing.

'No.' She kept her face lowered, almost sick with longing. How terrible to be committed to one man and only eighteen years old. What did he want with her?

'Caroline, look at me.'

She formed the one word with difficulty. 'Why?'

'Because I can't stand much more of this. Neither can you.'

She looked up then into his haunting light eyes and as she did so, he caught her up in his arms and carried her back to the other room.

'Would you believe me if I said I love you?'

'No.' He had her with him in the armchair, her head tilted back against his shoulder.

'What *would* you believe?' He looked down at her lovely, creamy face. 'That I've been nearly mad these past months? That when I caught up with you I swore I'd use violence?'

'You already have,' she pointed out.

'No.' Kiall lowered his head and kissed her throat.

Nothing could cool the fire that ran through her at his touch. 'Haven't you forgotten something?' she said shakily. 'You sent *me* away.'

'I wanted you to forget me altogether.'

'How?' she asked, the pain slashing through her. 'How was I supposed to do that?'

'I was wrong.' He traced his fingers over her pure profile. 'Loving you was the most natural thing in the world. Maybe it's wrong, I don't know, but I can't let you go. You know it—I know it.' A faint tremor ran through his strong hand. It caught her under the chin, turning her mouth up to him.

'Kiall.' She was crying without knowing it and he gathered her to him with a pulverising passion, kissing her with such hunger it increased her own craving.

'Let me hold you, love you,' he begged.

'For how long?'

'My poor foolish baby, for ever. For all the years of our lives. We own each other.'

'And what about who I am?'

'You're mine,' he said harshly. 'You're yourself.'

'I wasn't sure you could love,' Caroline said brokenly. 'I couldn't bear it for us to be together like this only for you to recoil afterwards.'

'Darling,' he said, enclosing her breasts gently, 'I love you. I knew it at once, though I tried to deny it. I'm prepared to do anything to keep you in my life.'

'What as, especially?' She tilted back her head, staring up at him.

'All you could be,' he said, a kind of severity on his dark face. 'My wife.'

Her hand came up to touch the rasping satin of his cheek, her fingers moving until they rested against the cleft in his chin. 'I want a son with a chin like that,' she said slowly, each word making her heart quiver.

'Do you?' Kiall bent his head and kissed her so deeply she felt she would faint away with the exquisite sweetness. Everything she ever wanted, come together in one man. 'I've taken you a hundred times in my imagination,' he said against her mouth. 'You're so completely right.'

'Danae showed me a ring.' She stopped his caressing hand.

'A ring?' He jerked up his head, a brittle little smile on his mouth. 'And of course she talked you into believing I gave it to her?'

'Everything pointed towards it being the truth.'

'Except I never at any time contemplated marrying Danae.'

'You made love to her.'

'So?' His sparkling eyes were ironic. 'I've made love to lots of women. You're the only one I've ever wanted to devour. You're the only one I want to keep beside me to love and protect. I guess I'm a one-woman man.

In fact, I'm damned sure of it.'

Caroline turned his palm against her mouth and kissed it, so enormously excited it must have shown in her face. 'And your aunt? Your family?'

Kiall ran his hand through her silky hair. 'Thea has decided to stay in England,' he said bluntly. 'She has her own pride. There's no place for her at Maralaya any more. She's a rich woman. She'll have little trouble readjusting. As for my mother, she loves me. She only wants what will make me happy. She was always on Deborah's side. Did you know that?'

'I have something to show you.' Caroline went to push herself up, but he held her by the waist.

'Show me later. After I've made love to you.'

'Now.' She put her fingers against his, so he relaxed his hold.

'All right.' He forced himself to let her go, watching her as she walked gracefully into the other room.

Within a minute she was back, holding a leather-bound book in her hand.

'What is it?' Sensitive to her every mood, Kiall knew she was upset.

'My mother's diary.'

'Give it to me and come here.' He put out his hand imperatively and she curled across his lap, staying like that while the long minutes ticked away.

'My God!' he muttered.

By the time he was finished, she was crying—healing tears for the past.

'Darling,' he shifted her even closer to his vibrant body, sighing softly against her hair, 'why didn't you let me know? Didn't you know how much it meant to me?'

'I didn't think you wanted me anyway.'

'Little fool!' There was passion, tenderness, on his

beautiful, stern mouth. 'May I show my mother this? She felt so strongly that Deborah was blameless.'

'Yet she loved her Martin after all.'

'Don't brood, darling,' he said rather sombrely, 'it will do us no good.'

'Then kiss me,' Caroline whispered. 'Make. me forget everything except how much I love you.'

Kiall tightened his hold on her, one hand going to the zipper of her dress. 'From now on, when you kiss me,' he said exultantly, 'you'll *never* run away.'

ROMANCE

Variety is the spice of romance

Each month, Mills & Boon publish new romances. New stories about people falling in love. A world of variety in romance – from the best writers in the romantic world. Choose from these titles in December.

DESIRE   Charlotte Lamb
BRIDE FOR A CAPTAIN   Flora Kidd
WITH A LITTLE LUCK   Janet Dailey
NORTH OF CAPRICORN   Margaret Way
TEMPORARY MARRIAGE   Kay Thorpe
CAPTURE A STRANGER   Lilian Peake
RACE FOR REVENGE   Lynsey Stevens
CORAL CAY   Kerry Allyne
HEAVEN ROUND THE CORNER   Betty Neels
AT FIRST GLANCE   Margaret Pargeter

On sale where you buy paperbacks. If you require further information or have any difficulty obtaining them, write to: Mills & Boon Reader Service, PO Box 236, Thornton Road, Croydon, Surrey CR9 3RU, England.

Mills & Boon
the rose of romance

FREE-an exclusive Anne Mather title, MELTING FIRE

At Mills & Boon we value very highly the opinion of our readers. What <u>you</u> tell us about what you like in romantic reading is important to us.

So if you will tell us which Mills & Boon romance you have most enjoyed reading lately, we will send you a copy of MELTING FIRE by Anne Mather – absolutely FREE.

There are no snags, no hidden charges. It's absolutely FREE.

Just send us your answer to our question, and help us to bring you the best in romantic reading.

CLAIM YOUR FREE BOOK NOW

Simply fill in details below, cut out and post to: Mills & Boon Reader Service, FREEPOST, P.O. Box 236. Croydon, Surrey CR9 9EL.

The Mills & Boon story I have most enjoyed during the past 6 months is:

TITLE _____

AUTHOR_____ BLOCK LETTERS, PLEASE

NAME (Mrs/Miss) _____ EP4

ADDRESS _____

_____

_____ POST CODE _____

Offer restricted to ONE Free Book a year per household. Applies only in U.K. and Eire.
CUT OUT AND POST TODAY – NO STAMP NEEDED

Mills & Boon
the rose of romance